Sinbad
the New Voyages

AIRSHIP 27 PRODUCTIONS

AN AIRSHIP 27 PRODUCTION

Sinbad-The New Voyages Volume One

Sinbad and the Island of the Simurgh © 2012 Nancy Hansen
Sinbad and the Sapphire of the Djinn © 2012 by I. A. Watson
Sinbad and the Voyage to the Land of the Frozen Sun © 2012 by Derrick Ferguson

Published by Airship 27 Productions
www.airship27.com
www.airship27hangar.com

Interior illustrations © 2012 Ralf Van Der Hoeven
Cover illustration © 2012 Bryan Fowler

Editor: Ron Fortier
Associate Editor: Charles Saunders
Production and design by Rob Davis.

ISBN-13: 978-0615695891
ISBN-10: 0615695892

Printed in the United States of America

10 9 8 7 6 5 4 3 2 1

SINBAD
the New Voyages
TABLE of CONTENTS

In search of a magical navigation device, Sinbad and his crew seek out a legendary creature on a fabled lost island filled with danger.

Attempting to save the benevolent Caliph's life, Sinbad and his crew take on a race against a clockwork mage and his airship.

Sinbad and the crew of the Blue Nymph embark on a voyage to a dangerous island pursued by a beautiful and deadly witch; their mission to save the world from her clutches.

SINBAD and the ISLAND of the SIMURGH

By Nancy Hansen

Sinbad El Ari leaned back against the tapestry covered wall and his ever restless blue eyes scanned the interior of the waterfront tavern. If one wanted to fill out a new crew, this was a good place to hunt for men eager to be at sea. He had stopped in again for the afternoon to waste a few dinars on weak drink and easy women in order to send several additional men to Omar, who was waiting down at the docks. Dressed in his finest clothing and turban, he appeared successful and confident, which always lured in more prospects.

His previous crew—what remained of it—had been paid well for their silence. Most had willingly taken their leave of the crazy captain of the Blue Nymph and his propensity for sailing them into the lands of monsters and mayhem. A good quarter of them had died on that last venture, and while that meant more coin to those who survived, even experienced sailors spook easily. Sinbad knew he would have to start with many green recruits again.

His eyes grew half lidded as the aromatic smoke from a hookah being shared at the next table filled the air. The sound of hand cymbals came from the dance floor, and all eyes turned to see. His did too, but the dancer cavorting in veils and bells was well past the bloom of youth, and he'd had enough of women for a while. He smiled though; his teeth straight and gleaming white between the dark mustache and neatly pointed beard on a face the deepest, richest shade of the sweet, plump Moroccan dates that traded so well. He sat back to watch the show, laughing at the fools throwing their money down, hoping for a stolen kiss or some whispered hints of forbidden delights from a woman who for many was old enough to be their mother. What drink and lust did to men was always entertaining!

An elderly blind man sat two tables over, his topi and ajrak marking him as one of the Sindh. His voice was high pitched and wavering, his palsied hands shook with the tremors of age, but his mind was clear and he still spoke knowledgeably about life on the water.

"Oh yes, oh yes," he said, gesturing wildly, "We found many exotic places with our magickal star chasers. It is not a figment of my age, because I still remember them well. I just cannot recall how to make them. You have to understand, such knowledge is above me, for after all, I was only a sailor, not a scientist or the captain. But I saw them working, and we went ashore in lands you would never dream of. Uncharted islands and mysterious continents would simply appear out of the misty brine! Men of strange origin, creatures most fantastic—I have seen them all, certainly. Sometimes, we barely escaped with our lives, but it was always worth it, for such treasures we found, with plenty for all to share! It is why I am able to support myself in my old age without begging on the street. Before I lost my sight, I had seen many things you could never imagine in a million years because of this wondrous device."

The men sitting with him gave each other meaningful looks, and a couple shook their heads. Two of the older ones got up and left. They obviously did not believe the elder one was fully in control of his wits anymore.

That conversation garnered Sinbad's full attention, for he also had seen many wonders in the world. It would be interesting to find out exactly what such an aged and experienced sailor did know, so he decided to gain an audience with him. A serving girl in dreadlocks and a sarong strolled by and Sinbad clapped his hands together rapidly. She sauntered over, smiling broadly, one hand on an ample hip, waiting in a provocative pose, her voice low and sultry toned.

"What can I bring you, captain?"

"What does this grandfather drink tonight?" He inclined his head toward the elderly man.

"Oh, just the spiced chai. He is too old for strong liquor." Her smile showed a gold tooth and dimpled her cheeks. She was comely, but young.

Sinbad nodded gravely. "I see. Bring him a fresh cup, with my compliments for his venerable knowledge. If he so wishes, I would join him for a while, and bask in his tales." He flipped her a coin and she caught it expertly, tucking it carefully into her skimpy top, making sure he noticed exactly where it rested. But Sinbad had already turned his attention away, and was once again focused on the conversation at the old sailor's table.

The younger people sitting with the venerable man gradually moved off laughing, until he sat alone, smacking his toothless gums and rocking lightly, muttering to himself. His tea came, and he nodded that he would be delighted to speak to someone willing to sit with him and listen with interest. Sinbad was already on his feet, towering over the girl when she brought him the message.

"The old one would greatly enjoy your company, captain," she said. Before she could wheedle another tip, he strode past her, eager to sit down and pick the man's brain.

They spoke until late in the evening, and then the elderly one shambled out, tapping his way forward with his walking stick. Sinbad left shortly after he did, making his way down to the docks; a tall, muscular, self-confident man who had a lot on his mind, though those ever alert blue eyes scanned the surroundings for trouble and his scimitar and curved dagger would come easily to hand if it somehow found him.

❀ ❀ ❀

That night, aboard The Blue Nymph, Sinbad called a meeting of his most trusted associates.

"So I take it you did not find us any more crew members today," a short and burly middle aged man said sourly, his arms crossed upon his barrel chest as he glared up at his captain. Of all the men with whom Sinbad had ever sailed, only Omar was bold enough to openly challenge him. He was a knowledgeable sailor and a capable master of both ship and crew. He would be forgiven his lack of deference for he spoke the truth in a way that balanced his captain's impulsive ideas.

Sinbad's smile was rueful, "No I did not Omar, but I did find out something very interesting. That is why I called you all here." He looked around the small group, noting that once again, Tishimi and Ralf had been prompt to report but Henri was just then hustling down the docks toward them, his bow over his shoulder and quiver on his back. He would be punished for being slow, likely losing part of his wine ration once they were at sea and he could no longer smuggle a bottle aboard. In a port town, you could find almost anything for a price, and the fast talking, nimble fingered Delacrois was prone to helping himself whenever possible.

"You're late again," Sinbad said flatly with his blue eyes narrowed as the agile man leapt halfway up the planking between dock and deck without regard for the footing.

"I have a good reason, Capitaine," the wiry man in dagged-edged hood, tunic and leathers said with a small bow of deference to his superiors and companions.

"He always seems to find some good reason to show up last," Ralf Gunarson said in his deep growling voice with no trace of the smirk showing beneath his luxurious golden beard. Thick muscled arms were crossed on his massive, leather clad chest, while eyes as transparent blue and cold as the glaciers of his Norse homeland rested on the shorter man with glittering intensity. Ralf was an enormous man. Taller and broader than any of them—including Sinbad—he always seemed fierce and imposing, even without the massive double-bitted axe casually stuck in his belt or his sword in hand. His threatening appearance often hid a wry sense of humor, for even now he was smiling. Henri always had a lie ready, and they were generally quite entertaining tales.

"I can explain it all," the little man with the mop of brown hair and thick mustache began, his hands up like a supplicant. "You see, there was this lady, and she said she knew something about a man who had a map…"

There was a collection of groans, for they had all heard this one before.

"Perhaps we should just get on with this before we need to spend another week at anchor talking about Henri's intimate activities," Tishimi Osara proposed in her quiet, precise voice. A slender but strong and calloused left hand slid between the cord wrapped hilts of her katana and wakizashi, while her right alternately clenched into a fist and opened to stretch. She shifted on her feet with the natural born balance of a dancer who became a warrior. In the form fitting black silks and woven straw sandals, she moved with feline grace and lithe power that flowed from head to toe. As usual, she had little to say, but when the female samurai spoke, they had learned to listen to her counsel.

"All right then," Sinbad started and he caught each eye in turn. "You are all my most trusted companions, so I will ask you all to listen carefully before you respond. Today I have learned of something that I previously did not know existed. Suppose I told you that we could build a device that would allow us to navigate to lands so uncharted they lie virtually undiscovered? Lands where treasure is everywhere! Would you come with me?"

There was a short silence, and then Omar began to laugh uproariously. "Forgive me Sinbad, but I would say you have either been too far into your cups or someone's hookah contained more than Turkish tobacco!"

That got a quick laugh out of Henri and a chuckle from both Sinbad and Ralf, though Tishimi only rolled her green eyes and shifted on her feet restlessly.

"No, it is true my loyal friends," Sinbad told them, shaking his head and flashing that dazzling smile that had won the heart of many a maid. "I have spoken to one of the oldest Sindhi sailors that I have ever met alive, and a very prosperous man he is, even at his advanced age. He talked of a device that when placed on the prow of a ship brought clearing weather with good winds and no fog or storms, so that one can sail to the places previously unknown without misfortune and find them readily."

"What device is this you speak of?" said Omar in a scoffing tone and his arms went up and out to illustrate his confusion. "I have stood on a deck since I was old enough to work, and I have not heard of any such thing! I do not believe it can exist! He must have been feeble minded with age."

"No, I found his mind quite clear," Sinbad said with his arms crossed on his chest and the beginning of a scowl darkening his blue eyes.

Ralf, whose people were also great mariners, shook his shaggy head in agreement with Omar. "Hah! The Norse would never have use for such a waste of time and effort. If you know the movement of the sun, the stars, the sea and the birds, you can go anywhere, even in one of these clumsy wooden whales." He glanced out over the port, at the ships anchored and docked, and snorted. "You don't need this device Sinbad; you need a faster ship!"

Sinbad's blue eyes turned stormy, appearing as indigo as the tightly furled sailcloth above him, an indication that the affront had been too great.

"There is nothing slow or clumsy about The Blue Nymph," he said in am outraged tone, one hand on the hilt of his sword. A twitch below his eye was the only other warning that this was a subject that was not open to differing opinions. Omar also looked incensed, and the pugnacious little man was red-faced and almost spitting in his anger at the tall Viking, but he would not speak while the captain was in charge, though he too fingered the hilt of his blade.

Ralf did not miss the threat in both men, for he was a cocky young warrior from a land where men were used to battling for their honor. Before he knew it, the axe was in his hands. The silence grew deadly as the tension between them mounted. Omar he could take out quickly; Sinbad however was a very capable fighter. But Ralf knew he was a stranger in a foreign country, and these were his only comrades in arms. It was not worth ruining their friendship over insulting a ship, but he was a proud man, so he stood his ground.

Henri was already backing up, ready to grab his bow and beat feet out of there. Tishimi's arresting green eyes went from one man to another as she settled herself on the balls of her feet, ready to defend her captain with her characteristic lightning speed slashes. As long as she bore the sword with her father's soul entwined in the metal, she believed she would not die, even against the powerful Norse giant.

Three against one was not bad odds, except two of these three were incredibly skilled and favored by their own gods. So the son of Gunar shrugged it off and shoved the axe back in his belt.

"All right, so I still don't speak the language well enough to make myself clear. This is a big ship; it rides low in the water compared to those that I have known. The drag makes it slower, but that doesn't make it a bad vessel, just different. Do I need to explain my words any further?"

Sinbad understood proud men well and he let it go. Ralf was a good man in a fight and he could carry twice as much plunder as any other. "No my large friend, I think you've said enough." Everyone relaxed.

"So what is...," Henri's fingers waggled in the air, "this, eh... miracle contrivance—and how do we get one?"

"Well, you see, that is the thing," Sinbad said in his best wheedling tone. "We have to build it ourselves, and unfortunately the old man could not tell me all the materials we would need. There is some specific balance of a certain kind of metal shavings along with a particular type of crystal, both of which are bound by a very clear resin that comes from someplace he couldn't remember; and something about a lodestone, and a copper spiral. The rest he had forgotten, but he told me that when properly prepared, it became like jewels of many layers and each component part worked with the others to achieve an alchemic reaction that reads the heavens and brings smooth sailing. When they put it in the eyes of their figurehead, everyone aboard the ship could see things that weren't there."

"That's witchery!" Henri said, and backed off, crossing himself. Omar had also gone pale, the blood beneath his swarthy skin drained away.

"That is something we should not do, not know about, not speak of!" the normally exuberant mate said quickly, his dark eyes having gone wide with fear. "Sinbad you are flirting with evil! Allah will punish us and I will not allow it on this ship–"

"Oh, I see. So you are now the captain?" Sinbad said with a glare.

"No, of course not! Forgive me Sinbad... I just... this is..."

"So we're off on another adventure," Ralf said matter-of-factly. "Where are we going?"

"To the island of the Simurgh," said Sinbad said confidently, naming the ancient winged creature which possessed the knowledge of three ages of earth. "If anyone knows what materials we need to build such a device, that one will."

Omar looked shocked, but "Sinbad—that is a most a dangerous place! And you cannot go there without bringing it a gift! Anything that creature would desire would be worthy of the Caliph's treasury. We have no such riches!"

Sinbad had already turned and began walking away, but he stopped and said, "We have more than you think Omar. Let me do the worrying, you get the ship provisioned and ready, and deal with the crew. We sail on the afternoon tide."

With that, he leapt lightly to the dock and was soon lost in the darkness. As the others left to pack their things and say their farewells, Henri was still pestering his companions.

"Can't someone tell me why we are going to ask for help from a big bird?"

"Don't question the captain, Gaul man, just bring plenty of arrows with you," Ralf advised as they parted company.

The little archer stood and watched his giant companion disappear into the night, and then hustled off to say a long goodbye to a pair of very friendly carter's daughters.

❋ ❋ ❋

When they left port at midday, the oars were out until The Blue Nymph was clear of the harbor and had turned with the wind. Men scrambled around on deck, as the sheet was unfurled and made fast. Eventually the snapping and bellying of it began to catch the wind and dragged them out to sea once more.

"South by southwest, captain's orders!" was repeated up and down the line.

As always at the beginning of a voyage, Omar was busy stomping from one end of the deck to another, shouting orders to the men and shaking his head over these ignorant fools. He made sure the oar master and drummer set the proper pace and the rigging men stood at the ready to swing the beam and lash the sail. He was too involved with getting underway to fret much now.

Ralf and Henri were both hung-over, but other than being pale and quieter than normal, the Norseman accepted his pounding head and roiling stomach stoically and helped the crew wherever he could. Henri however was leaning over the aft rail shaking and retching his guts out; sick from copious amounts of wine with too much rich food, and exhausted from many hours of frenetic lovemaking the night before. His dark rimmed brown eyes showed a lack of sleep, and he huddled in a useless heap in between bouts of nausea.

Tishimi remained alone on foredeck, out of the way, where the new Arabic sailors aboard would not find her female presence as offensive. She had spent her night resting and so had been up with the dawn. She had set aside her weapons and began going through a set of silent drills and postures, readying her body and mind for the challenges ahead. Sinbad watched her from his position at the tiller, for he always insisted on piloting the ship out into the open water at the beginning of a voyage. The samurai was an enigmatic woman, but one he was content to leave to her own devices. The blades she swung were sharp and fast, and in her capable hands, they sang a song of blood and honor. Such companions as he had were rare, and he thanked Allah for their loyalty.

"It will be a worthwhile trip," he reassured himself as the ship began to cut through the waves. "May fortune smile upon us once more." The island of the Simurgh was not far off; a month's journey at best, but it was well out of the shipping lanes, in the opposite direction that most merchants and traders took, for none cared to pass very closely. Besides the reefs and shoals around it, the area had a menacing reputation for sea serpents and other strange creatures that were said to be the guardians of the ancient beast. It would not be easy to reach it, but with luck and courage, it should prove to be a most enlightening journey.

The weather was reasonably good, with only one short storm that lashed the decks with wind, rain, and salt spray, and tossed the men around for a day and part of the night. Several days beyond that, they encountered a pirate vessel. It was just before they reached the narrow passage that would take them to the Arabian Gulf, or what Tishimi's people called 'the Red Sea'.

"A Kytherian, of course. Have them row hard, so that we stay well ahead," Sinbad told Omar. "We'll outrun them."

"Bah, let them catch up," Ralf insisted, testing a thumb against his axe blade. "I have not killed anyone in many weeks!"

Sinbad clapped a hand on his broad shoulder. "We have business elsewhere my friend. You're still a young man. I'm sure you'll have plenty of other opportunities to prove your battle worthiness."

He had no idea how prophetic those words would be!

On the rocky summit of a small island that time had passed by, was a tall, flat topped promontory. In a great stone temple there, built eons ago by men who were barely human, a large creature slept away most of its current life. This day however, it had awakened and stirred. A huge head with the snout and split lip of a camel but the lengthy muzzle of a dog, and eyes that were as old and spirited as a dragon but contained the wisdom of owls, came out from under a wing of iridescent plumage tipped in bronze. A tail fanned and shook out, and talons flexed and relaxed as it stood and stretched, looking out far to sea, beyond the sight of any mortal being. The voice was quiet and wheezy, but it carried far.

"They come! Men come from the sea, to our land. They have questions, and I have answers. But are they worthy? Time will tell."

It moved out of the temple to the edge of the precipice and craned its neck skyward. Feathers of many hues on a long, strong neck pulsed and ruffled, while long fur-like quills stood out from over its amber eyes, giving it a quizzical expression. It nodded sagely.

"They will be tested, oh yes," the creature said with a bob of its great head. "The trials will be cruel and there will be much hardship; but then, no knowledge is without its price."

It paced the perimeter of the flat topped space occupied by the temple and cocked its head. Beneath the ruffled feathers, an ear opening picked up the sound of a voice too far off for any other creature to hear. A rueful smile spread across the cloven lips, showing teeth as white as snow and sharp as knives.

"Welcome, Sinbad El Ari, ever restless son of the sea. Perhaps you will live to find what you seek, and may it be worth the price paid!"

It suddenly stretched its neck and let out a single, ringing, reverberating cry, something that made fangs show, fur rise, and scales shake all over the island, for it was a call to guard and defend.

They were well out of the shipping lanes when the craggy cliffs of the island of the Simurgh appeared on the horizon, appearing briefly now and then between the shifting curtain of fog and mist surrounding it. The water around them ran swift and fast, with a bit of a rip and huge swells. It was impossible to see what lurked beneath the turbulent surface.

Sinbad stood on deck, his cerulean gaze fixed on the faint outline of the long-avoided land between the mists. This was where he hoped to find the answers to his ever ongoing quest for fresh sights to see and new lands to explore.

"We need to move farther in," he said.

"There are dangerous reefs here, Sinbad," Omar warned him.

His captain turned to him, his eyes narrowed in a thoughtful look as restless fingers stroked his pointed beard. "I know, but we can't send in a smaller boat from this far out to sea. Let's circle the island, see how close we can get before we set anchor. Then we will think about a landing party."

"I'll get the oarsmen going," said Omar with a frustrated sigh, and he stomped off muttering to himself. After a brief grin in his cantankerous companion's direction, Sinbad's attention was riveted once again on the island itself, which like a veiled dancer, only allowed tantalizingly brief glimpses of its hidden assets. He was so involved with studying it; he never noticed that the dolphins which usually swam alongside them had suddenly left, and that there was a strange wake following closely behind theirs. In fact, it wasn't until something bumped the keel hard enough to be felt that the changes got his attention.

"Omar, we've struck shallows here," Sinbad called out sternly as he headed back toward the rudder man.

"That is impossible!" the short, squat man insisted and he came running. "We have been sounding all the way, and it is still plenty deep here! I do not understand why Allah trials me so!"

"Well, we've hit something," Sinbad said with a frown, as there was another bump on the port side, cracking a couple of oars and making the men below decks shout in anxiousness. Sinbad stalked back over that way and passed Tishimi, who was staring intently at the waves. She grabbed his arm.

"Sinbad, there is a creature moving beneath the water. It is swimming with us."

"It's likely a whale," he said quietly but she shook her head, not taking those sharp green eyes off the water.

"It is no whale, or any sea creature I know. Long and narrow body, long neck, small head, and four flippers. You see?" She pointed.

He peered at the water for a moment, but then there was a piercing shriek and a string of curses in Norse from the aft of the ship!

Sinbad and Tishimi whirled in unison just in time to see the rudder man lifted off the deck by a mottled skinned, long necked beast of the deep. Most of the creature was still underwater, but the unfortunate man's head and neck were already engulfed in its huge maw. Great curved teeth the size of daggers sank into his chest, his lifeblood spurting in runnels down his torso as fists still spasmodically pounded the jaws and his feet kicked feebly in the air.

As they ran, drawing their weapons, Ralf Gunarson was already on the scene, fearlessly hacking away at the thing's long neck, though his axe rebounded off, leaving no more than surface damage that barely oozed the ichors of the flesh within. The creature withdrew and writhed with discomfort, tossing the now limp and decapitated body of the dead man back onto the deck to go after the Viking. The neck reared back like a snake, and it hissed before lunging at him so fiercely, it shoved against The Blue Nymph and pushed her forward. Ralf lost his balance, and slipping in the blood and spray, he fell backward onto the deck, dropping his axe. He rolled over and into the fall, snatching up his weapon again as the creature snapped at him, though it couldn't quite reach him without heaving its bulk out of the water.

Henri had set up a ways from Ralf, down on one knee, arrow nocked and moving with the swaying head as he tried to get in another shot. The skin of the thing was far too thick, and his broadheads had barely scratched the surface before dropping uselessly into the water.

"Mon Dieux, stay out of the way a moment Ralf, *vous grande imbécile!"* he yelled and launched another one, which sailed over the Viking and landed squarely in a large yellow eye the size of a tavern trencher. The beast shook its head like a wet dog and bellowed something between a roar and an ear piercing scream of pain before backing off, rolling sideways, and diving deep.

In the water all around The Blue Nymph, similar heads popped up, at least a dozen of them. Several hissed defiantly. Henri took aim and hit two more of them the same way before they all dove under and disappeared. "It is the most vulnerable spot," he explained to Ralf, when the big man rejoined him. The Viking only grunted, but thumped him on the back nearly hard enough to knock the wind from the smaller man, who staggered forward before regaining his balance. Between comrades, that was enough praise.

There was a reverberating scraping noise from the underside where they had just grazed the top of a reef while the big boat was rudderless. Sinbad grabbed the tiller again, and muscles straining, wrestled it back under control. He turned them away, keeping the big ship from yawing too much and ending up foundered.

"Bring that sail around, and oarsmen twice as long strokes on the starboard side. Turn and take us farther out to sea, Omar, and quickly," he ordered as men rushed to do his bidding.

Ignoring some dark looks from the deck crew, Ralf and Henri dragged the headless body of the former helmsman away, and set it under one of the smaller landing boats. What was left of the man would be wrapped in his blanket and consecrated to the sea later, before sundown, as was the

...it hissed before lunging at him...

custom of his people. But not here, where one of those great beasts, or the scavenging sharks that followed them, would gorge on his remains.

"I can see this is going to be an interesting trip," Henri said quietly once they had rejoined Tishimi in watching the area near the reef where the snake-necked monsters hunted, which now receding behind them.

No one argued with him, for even with the blood and gore on the deck sluiced off, and the headless body wrapped in the blanket and being sewn into sail cloth, the horror of that first encounter with the guardians of the island of the Simurgh remained. The attack had come suddenly, and with vicious savagery. There was a lot of unhappy muttering about exposing men to excessive danger without warning them before they signed on. Omar's bamboo cane was slapping his hand as he stomped back and forth between stations, a frown creasing his brow beneath his head covering, making his heavy features even homelier.

"One wonders what other vile secrets that place holds," Tishimi said quietly, one hand on a slim hip and the other caressing the hilts of her sheathed weapons as she watched the island receding behind them.

"We'll find out soon enough," Ralf rumbled, and they all sighed.

They anchored out at sea for the night, though a double watch was kept and lanterns burned on all sides. There were no more incidents, but the dawn showed the possibility of a storm coming on. The thin squall line on the western horizon was likely just coming off the African coast, but it was moving rapidly and would be upon them by midday. The clouds looked ominously dark and angry.

"This is not monsoon season!" Omar said with suspicion. "This weather plays more tricks on me than my third wife!"

"Yes, I suspect this is unnatural, too. No matter, we need to be on the lee side of the island in case this gets serious," Sinbad insisted, for the wind was already playing with the sail as they set the oarsmen back to work. "Let's go around it—farther out this time—and then see if we can find a safe way in."

"Let us hope there are no more of those long necked things around there," Omar said with a shudder. "Allah must have had an off day when he created that one!"

For some reason that bold statement in the face of fear made Sinbad laugh as he went off to gather his warrior companions to his side for an impromptu conference.

"We have a storm coming in, and must reach some sort of sheltered spot where it is safe to anchor. Most of the crew will be busy rowing or trimming sail, so I cannot spare them as spotters. Yet I need all the eyes and ears I can get to keep watch for any further problems as well as a safe anchorage that might serve as protection. Most of these men have little experience with the unknown, but you three have sailed with us for some time now, so I trust you more. We will have to be on the far side of that island to withstand this storm, and I have no idea what lurks there. Please, be on your guard for anything that looks suspicious, or changes in the color of the water which can mean reefs below."

"We will do our best for you, Sinbad," Ralf said, pounding a fist to his heart, and Henri and Tishimi copied that.

"Thank you, my loyal friends. I will take the aft watch, for I must steer in these harsh waters. Tishimi takes the foredeck, Ralf the seaward side, and Henri to port. Sing out loudly if you see anything."

They all assumed their positions, and from battle experience in strange waters, kept their eyes moving from sea to horizon to sky and back.

Ralf, who was now wearing his helm, baldric and sheathed sword, and had his big round wooden shield at his feet, was the first one to spot something amiss. "Sinbad!" he shouted. "There is something flying below the clouds. Entire flocks of some kind of bird."

"That is not unusual with storms," Sinbad called back loudly over the rising wind.

Henri, who had the sharpest eyes, wandered over. "Sinbad, these birds have arms as well as legs and wings!"

"There is no such thing," Sinbad insisted as he looked behind him. Not only were the roiling clouds much closer, but beneath and before them were a solid mass of small fluttering forms. With their upright posture, they looked more like small flying people than birds. Their wings were the wrong shape and construction to be avian, rounded like moths, but ribbed like fish fins. It was curious, and there were so many of them, they clouded the sky before the storm, their echoing little voices calling plaintively in words no one could understand.

"Djinni!" yelled several of the crew, and they began fervent prayers of salvation.

"Get back to your work," said a very angry first mate, and he spared no back, legs, or buttocks from his cane.

"They are gaining on us!" Henri warned.

"Omar, get me a helmsman over here and post some other spotters around the sides!" Sinbad demanded. "Full sail, all oars out; we are getting around this infernal island!" He pulled forth his blade, a signal to arms for his companions. As he turned to face the incoming horde there was a look of grim determination and just the trace of a calculating smile on Sinbad's brown face. The wave of tiny beings circled the ship and began to spiral down, some of them cackling with delight, their wings making a peculiar vibrating buzz.

"I don't like the look of this!" said Henri as he shoved his bow end beneath a foot and strung it hurriedly. "They sound very hungry."

"At least they're smaller than you are, so they will take only little bites," Ralf said critically, while testing the edges of his axe blades with a thumb and keeping an eye on the leading dozen or so. He decided the reach of the broad sword would be more effective, and unsheathed that with a ringing sound of good metal.

"But there are far more of them, than *moi*," Henri countered as he nocked an arrow and took aim.

Tishimi had joined them, and she had fastened her glossy black hair into a high topknot with just the sides hanging down, so that it was out of her eyes. Both her weapons were in hand already and her green eyes were narrowed to slits as she squinted into the distance. "These are evil spirits of the unconsecrated dead of the open waters; I have seen them in my meditations. They come to steal more souls." She was already taking a spread legged battle stance, making sure she had enough room around her to freely swing both blades.

"Then the Gaul is safe at least, for he has no soul," Ralf commented wryly as he hefted his sword and shield. "I've seen the way he carries on ashore, and no one bound for Valhalla would do such things with maids barely out of diaper cloths."

Henri laughed at that as he let fly an arrow, instantly drawing and nocking another as the two little bodies it pierced fell screaming into water. "You're just jealous of my prowess with the jeune filles. Big fierce ogre that you are, they run away because they are afraid your oversize weapon will split them in two." He smiled at his own double entendre as he spitted several more.

"Men are such pigs," Tishimi said with distaste as she crossed her blades and then raised them, one at shoulder height and the other head high, never taking her intense green eyed gaze off of the incoming flock.

"I won't argue with that!" Ralf laughed even harder as he took an experimental swing to get the feel of an overhead fight. "Come closer little sky rats, my sword has been dry for far too long."

The nearer they got, the uglier the small creatures appeared. There was some variance in their features but for the most part they had vaguely human shapes with desiccated scaly skin of pale ochre stretched over a bony body with knobby knees and elbows. Feet and hands were tipped with long raking claws. They opened round mouths to screech, which showed sharply back-curved fangs behind rubbery lips. Their nostrils were mere slits, their eyes bulged with the multiple facets of insects, and indeed there were long, wispy antennae on some of them. The outstretched ribbed wings were in two pairs, upper and lower, and both sets fanned independently. As the cloud of them swooped downward, little dark pointed tongues flicked in and out repeatedly.

Within moments there was a blur of small bodies and vibrating wings swarming all over the people on deck, flapping in faces, nipping at hands and heads, biting necks and shoulders. Men who were brave in the face of storms and pirate raids ran shrieking and batting at themselves like harem girls beset by bees. Some of them went down beneath the weight of dozens of the creatures, flailing limbs and crying out in horror as they were overwhelmed and covered by small, greedy bodies. Many sets of fangs fastened into flesh, injecting anesthetizing venom that quickly made the victim catatonic.

Being taller, Ralf and Sinbad were already slashing and hacking at the multitude of creatures trying to bear them to the deck. The curved blade of the Sindhi captain proved to be more affective than the heavy, broad sword of the taller Viking, for it was easier to backswing and uppercut with. Still Ralf had a steadily accumulating pile of small chopped up bodies around him, for he was a fierce and determined fighter, never tiring, undaunted by the small bites and scratches that ran blood down his arms and shoulders and dripped onto his leather vest, the laces of which strained with his exertions.

Sinbad too had a few nips and his turban was askew, but he swung and parried like a madman, endlessly chopping and cleaving. Omar had joined him, as the smaller statured mate was fairly skilled with own broader curved blade. He took out those creatures which managed to slip by his taller companions, keeping them from getting a chance to hit a vital spot from below. As stout as he was, he fought incredibly well, though he grunted and puffed with the exertions as he hacked, slashed, stabbed and cleaved whatever got into his path.

Tishimi was a fury of animation as her dual swords piled small bodies all over the deck. She leapt and twirled, lunged and sliced; her form a blur of constant motion, making every single movement count. The twin highly polished blades she wielded made a whistling, whirring noise as they cut effortlessly through the flock, never missing a single opportunity to connect. Back and forth, up and down the deck she fought, throwing flashes like the lightning that snaked from the incoming clouds.

Having armed themselves, some of the crew joined the battle. No one fights like a Sindh protecting his own! The tide of events began to turn as the wind picked up to the point where even the little fiends of the air were having trouble staying aloft. Eventually they began to veer off, and there was a rousing cheer and cries of victory as the remainder of the flock moved away.

At least seven sailors were down. Two would never rise again; their bodies pale and looking almost mummified, drained of all fluid until the very tissues and organs within had shrunken into hard lumps. The living wounded and the dead men were quickly dragged below to be dealt with later, for the storm was almost upon them.

"We are going to get caught in the open in this infernal tempest!" Omar shouted to Sinbad as he wiped off his sword on his baggy pants leg and sheathed it. "We must find a safe place to drop anchor!"

Sinbad knew most of their losses had been in deck sailors, those who set and trimmed the sail. "We'll manage up here. Get as many men back to the oars as you can. Double and triple them up if you have to. Don't spare the lash—get us moving, Omar!" The squat little man ran down the deck, kicking small broken bodies away as he did, already shouting orders.

Sinbad was all captain now, and while the ship was being tossed, he was squarely in his element. He grinned like a madman as he wrestled with the tiller in the slapping waves and rising swells that were bobbing and heeling The Blue Nymph all around like an empty wine cask in a torrent.

"Ralf, lash down your weapons! I need you to manage the beam, for you have the strength of five men and the extra height to match. Tishimi and Henri, likewise you are needed, so stow your arms. You will have to be my trimmers, and climb the rigging to lash down that sail before it blows us over."

"But... but I am afraid of heights!" Henri complained as he tightly tied his bow and quiver in a sheltered spot.

Tishimi gave him a glowering look as she secured her own weapons. "We all will die here if the boat overturns because you could not find your manhood!"

"I know where *that* is," he grumbled as they began to climb opposite sides of the wet and slippery rigging, trying not get knocked off by loose flying lines or ends of sail flapping free. "I just want to live long enough to use it again."

"I think you have already used up several lifetime's worth by now," Ralf called up after him in his booming voice as he struggled and strained to keep the rigging leading to the crossbeam taut so it would not twist under the overloaded sail and rip free. He heaved and grunted, his whole body so corded with muscle he looked as stalwart as one of the mighty oaks of Britannia, where his clan used to go raiding.

Tishimi was light on her feet and athletic, so she made better time than Henri. Other than the bloody scratches on her face and hands, you would never know she had just fought a pitched battle. Reaching the top of the sail lashing before Henri, she called down to him.

"Hurry, it is blowing hard up here," she shouted as the skies opened up and wind driven rain began to come in sideways. It skewed the sail, which heeled The Blue Nymph so hard her decks were awash for a moment.

"I am trying, but my head spins," Henri called back.

"Your head will spin all over this deck if you don't stop complaining!" she goaded him.

Struggling to keep the rigging square, Ralf almost lost his footing in the deluge of water, but the giant of a man just grunted and yanked it down harder. "Come on Gaul, find your courage! Get up there with the girl and get that sail down before we capsize." Every muscle in his arms, shoulders and chest burned with the strain as he heaved and tugged, gritting his teeth and squinting against the stinging, wind swept spray.

Henri had finally reached the top of crossbeam too. He shouted down, barely heard above the howling winds, "Let go the lines my big friend, we will drag it in." He and Tishimi began tugging the sail up and furling it around the beam, crawling out cautiously, hanging on to the slippery length with legs and feet like monkeys as they frantically tried to control the sodden, flapping canvas and whipping lines long enough to lash it tight.

"Let's go!" Henri said as he began to carefully edge toward the middle rigging again. Tishimi signaled that she had heard him, but she had one more line to do, though it had a wind knot that refused to unravel. "Don't worry about that!" he called to her, but she was a bit of a perfectionist and set about it with teeth and nimble fingers.

Finally securing it, she began to slowly make her way back down when a loose loop became wrapped around her leg. She tried to tug free but then the entire mass slipped around the pole and she went sideways with it. She struggled a moment to hold on but the wind was against her and she began to slide off, her leg trapped beneath the lashing. She let go with her hands and managed to grab the rigging, but she couldn't kick herself free. The more the wind blew, the more it tightened around her leg, holding her fast.

"I am trapped!" she called to Henri, who was already halfway down. The winds were buffeting her around, and she was suddenly anxious of breaking free and falling to her death on the deck below.

The man from Gaul, in spite of his fear of heights, would not leave a comrade in danger. "Stay still, I'll come back for you," he shouted up, and breathing a prayer, he began the tedious climb up the rigging again.

He was only halfway to her when a huge gust of wind flattened him against the central mast, at the same time that it tore Tishimi's grip from the rigging, She screamed a warning below, thinking she would fall free and hit someone, but only dropped a few feet, though completely out of reach of anything she could grab onto.

Fortunately the rope tightened and twirled around her leg but it left her dangling upside down, held painfully by one calf and still at least four times her height from safety. There she swung in the fierce wind, out over the raging water and back in over the planked deck, unable to work her agile body upward and grab onto the line.

"Ralf, man the tiller! Tishimi, hold on, I'm coming!" Sinbad bellowed, as he raced across the slick surface to a better position where he could get to her.

"Sinbad!" Henri shouted down, as he finally inched his way above her. "Don't come up here, the rigging is tearing loose and it's too dangerous now for both of us to be on it. I can cut her free with almost enough slack to let her down if you can catch her!"

"Do it!" Sinbad insisted, and set himself up below. He was joined by Omar, who had a length of sailcloth bundled under one arm, and they briefly put their heads together.

The boat began to pitch sickeningly in the heavy waves, and Tishimi felt her leg would be torn from the socket with all the wild swinging.

"Hen-ree, let me go; no sense losing your life too," Tishimi insisted, her lighter voice lost to all but him as she craned her neck and tried to look up through the pouring rain. "My weight will pull you loose, and we'll both die."

"*Non, mon cherie,* I have yet to let a woman drag me down like that," he said with a lopsided smile as he began sawing at the rope above a knot, shaking water from his hair every so often. He kept calling down to her, for Tishimi was shivering with cold and fright, as the wind was wildly swinging her out and back. He was not much better off himself. "Besides, I have strong arms from all the shooting. If you were the Norseman, t'would be a different story. He weighs as much as ox, and is almost as smart. If he fell on his head, I would fear more for the deck!" He was a glad neither Ralf nor Sinbad could hear him, as he would undoubtedly pay for his glib statements later.

The last few strands sawn through, Henri lay against the cross beam and locked his legs around it, keeping a firm grip on the knotted end of the rope. Looking down through the wind driven rain to the heaving deck below, it seemed very far away and his stomach lurched. "OK, she is free, be ready," he said as he began to slowly pay out line.

Little by little, mere inches at a time; he lowered Tishimi until she was just above the heads of her friends, though still out of reach. With the straining efforts of the oarsmen, they were thankfully in safer and a bit less choppy waters by then. Ralf had lashed the tiller and joined them, but even he could not come near to touching her.

"I am out of line!" Henri yelled down. His hands were rope scarred and burning from the chafe of the rough and wet cording.

Sinbad, Ralf, and Omar took the cloth between them. "Keep it taut, but not too much, or she will bounce off," Omar warned, and the men adjusted their stance.

"All right Henri, let her go," Sinbad called out in the stentorian authoritative tone that had corrected many a young man new to the sea.

"Courage, *mon petite*! See you back on deck," he said and let go the rope. Tishimi tumbled herself as she fell, landing back first in the length of sail cloth, held fast by three straining men she trusted not to let her hit the deck below. They slowly lowered it until she could get to her feet. She undid the rope from her leg, and tossed it aside and stood upright.

"Thank you, my good friends," she said bowing to each one in turn.

"Well, I can see no one worries about moi," Henri said, as he too touched the deck at last.

"No, for you, I reserve the highest honor of all, Hen-ree," she said, and grabbing his face, she kissed him on the forehead.

He seemed a bit taken aback, but with a shrug he said, "*Bien*—but I was hoping at least on the lips, perhaps with a tickle of the tongue..."

"Men are such animals," she said with a lift of her little pointed chin, and they all laughed.

There was a general cheer from below when Omar went down to praise the tired crewmen for their hard work in getting them out of danger. The day was mostly over so they found a safe place at sea, far out from the reefs. The storm having spent most of its fury by then, it passed by to the northeast with no more than normal rain and gusting winds left. It was time to take stock of where they were, so they dropped the anchors, and a round of well watered drink was handed out before weary men went either to their bunks or back on watch for the evening.

"I am sure Allah allows for celebration as long as the mind remains clear and focused," Omar said to no one in particular.

"I wouldn't worry too much about becoming besotted from this baby piss," Ralf said with a snort.

The two men who had died were consecrated to the sea, along with another who passed during the storm. Of the four injured left, they all lay like the dead in their hammocks, lashed in lest they fall out as the ship still rocked a bit. Not a sound did they utter, but their staring eyes stayed open all night long with no blinking, their breathing became shallow and irregular, and their skin was white and as cold as ice on mountain tops. Their bodies remained emaciated, though their abdomens swelled alarmingly.

"I do not know what keeps them alive," Omar said to Sinbad in the captain's quarters as he gave his final report of the evening. His superior sat before his window watching the island disappearing in the dark as the sun set and night fell.

Sinbad was silent for a few moments, his impassive face in the flickering shadows appearing as if it was chiseled as of dark stone, backlit only by a single pan of tallow with a wick.

"It is what keeps any man alive, my friend," he said at last, turning his now enigmatic blue eyes back to Omar. "A will to go on."

❧ ❧ ❧

The next morning, they found the reef opening that Sinbad had hoped for on the southeastern side of the island. That area had the steepest terrain, with a semicircle of forbidding cliffs skirted by heavy jungle growth that led down to a crescent beach dotted with waving palms. The mists and fogs were thin there, as the winds from the south blew them away. There was a narrow channel in the outer reefs large enough for the Blue Nymph to navigate through with some care, and once in the quieter waters within that rocky barrier, they would be able to anchor safely and launch small

...they would...launch small boats to the shore.

boats to the shore.

"At last, we've caught a break," a more rested Sinbad said with a broad smile as he shaded his eyes and peered out over the water.

"I don't know, Sinbad," Ralf rumbled, shaking his head in disagreement so that his gathered lengths of blonde hair waved like a mare's tail behind him. "It's too easy."

"Hah! Now you sound like Omar—so negative! Relax, my giant friend, we'll soon have what we came here seeking," Sinbad answered with enthusiasm as the Blue Nymph began to turn and make her approach.

"I'll relax when this journey is over and we're out of these accursed waters," Ralf said abruptly as he stalked off to see if there was anything mildly resembling mead on board.

Two small landing crafts were prepared and dropped alongside of the Blue Nymph as Sinbad hand picked those who would go with him. "I'll take Ralf and Henri, and several of the crew who know jungles and mountains," he said to Omar. "But Tishimi is still limping and she should stay behind. Let her leg heal."

When she heard of that, she went directly to Sinbad, her face a mask of indifference though anger stirred in her green eyes. "I wish to know why I am being left out of this expedition," she said quietly with an edge to her voice.

Sinbad stood on the deck looking out at the island of the Simurgh, which was now far more visible through the thinner fogs and mists on that side. Normally he would not brook any trace of insolence or questioning of his orders from a member of his crew, but Tishimi had once saved his life. As always she had chosen her time well, catching him alone, and gave little outward indication that she had an issue with his command.

"I am sure you do," Sinbad answered just as quietly. He understood that the samurai's honor had been insulted. "That is a forbidding sight, don't you think?" he asked her, using his hands to outline the island's features as if he was an artist painting a mural. "The jungle beyond the beach is thick and will be hard to penetrate. We must climb the cliffs to get to the table land on top. Who knows what horrors lay in wait within those terrains?"

"Which is why you need me at your side. I can climb, and I fight well."

Sinbad turned to face her. "You are a great warrior, Tishimi Osara, and I am proud to have you as one of my crew, but you have been injured, and still walk with a limp," he reminded her gently. "It will only get worse the more you push yourself. That leg needs rest."

"I feel fine, I have little pain, and I do not fear monsters; I kill them. You forget, my captain—I cannot die in battle against the otherworldly beasts as long as I have my father's sword. I must go with you."

Sinbad knew when it was time to enforce his rank. "Perhaps *you* cannot be killed," he snapped, "But your comrades can die because they think you have their backs, though you will not reach them in time with that injured leg. Or they might fall from a cliff trying to save you when the leg gives out and you misstep. You will stay behind this time, and guard the ship, and there is no dishonor in that. These are strange waters, and I fear also for my crew who will be left behind as much as for those who accompany me. Now we will speak of this no longer, or I will have you confined to your quarters."

"Yes captain," she said coldly, and turned to walk off.

"Tishimi," he called, and she stopped and waited. She turned and he met her eyes, which were empty of all emotion. "Make sure you guard my ship and its crew well. The Blue Nymph is my life; it is the finest vessel I have ever sailed. I may never have another one this well fitted. I'm depending on you."

"I will do my best for you as always Sinbad," she said with a fist to her heart, and then walked away again.

❀ ❀ ❀

Threading their way through the reefs with long oars for paddling or poling, the two lightweight boats slipped along the surface right after dawn. They took weapons, and some casks with them for fresh water and fruit or whatever else could be scavenged. Sinbad carried a small sack over one shoulder, containing his 'gifts' for the Simurgh, should they be fortunate enough to reach it.

All eyes kept a close watch around them as they paddled quietly through the last reef opening and toward the beach itself. The tide was low; the water shallow and warm. It held many wonders within it, all of them creatures of normal dimensions. Even the reef sharks were small and shy.

"Perhaps we have passed the worst dangers," Henri said hopefully from where he sat in the middle of the lead boat that held Sinbad, two men and a wide-eyed orphan boy.

"I doubt it," Ralf rumbled from his position at the stern of the second boat, which he was helping to pole along from a seated position. "If this place was that easy to reach, everyone would be here."

"We will remain on our guard at all times." Sinbad cautioned the men with them as their light boats grated on the sand of the beach and they leapt out to pull them well ashore, above the high water mark. "Keep your blades easily at hand, and do not take anything for granted. We are strangers here, and have no idea what kind of wildlife this jungle holds. Ralf, you're with me and these three," he said, indicating the two grown men and the boy. "You two," he pointed to a couple of bulky, squat men carrying casks, "Go just far enough inland to find water and fresh food. Henri will accompany you for your protection as you work, and then the three of you come back and stand guard by the boats. My intention is that we will leave this island well before evening. I prefer to be back on board by sunset because we need daylight to get safely through the reef."

As they picked up their things and started off, Henri looked at Ralf and said, "*Bonne chance, mon ami!*" and stuck out his hand.

"Fight well, with honor, my friend," the big man countered, and gripped his forearm so hard it shut off the circulation. Then with his axe in his belt and a jaunty air of adventure, the Viking strode off to bring up the rear of his exploration party as they entered the jungle, cutting their way through. It seemed to close right up behind them, covering their trail and drowning out sounds, other than the bird and animal calls the men on the beach could hear above the restless waves.

"Let us go find that water and food and be done with this," Henri said to the other two men, who were staring at the jungle growth with some trepidation. "I spotted a freshet coming down the cliff over to the west as we were rowing in. There should be a clear pool at the base. Come, we will remain on the sand until we see it and then only hike in as far as we must. I will guide and guard you."

As they walked along the beach, they did not see the cold and appraising olive green eyes that watched them. There was a bit of rustling as a big head lifted up to see better, and a long forked tongue of bright yellow flicked out and back in, tasting the air. This was soft fleshed prey that did not move fast, so it signaled to others of its kind by low toned humming as a long, heavy, finely scaled body began to stalk slowly along on sharp clawed feet.

The sailors following the warrior with the bow on his shoulder were so busy conversing in their own language; they did not notice the shuffling and swaying of foliage along the jungle edge nearby. The tracking beasts paced the three men making their way toward the area where Henri had spotted a small waterfall. There would be one chance to cut them off, just before they entered the thicker growth. As they neared the point of contact, the creatures picked up speed and began to sidle along very quickly, surrounding the men on three sides to push them out onto the open beach where their kind ran well and there were few trees to climb.

❀ ❀ ❀

"This is hard work, Captain," a continually complaining man named Samad said, dropping his arm to his side. Omar would have whipped him for speaking up, but everyone was exhausted after half a day of making their way through the heavy growth. Sweat poured off all their bodies. Their swords in their respective scabbards to protect the edges, they were using machetes and sticks to make their way through the thick plants. The air was humid and somewhat rank with the smell of rotten vegetation in and around the pools they sometimes had to skirt. Wild warbling cries of some strange beast in the treetops and the fluttering of colorful butterflies and birds greeted them as they hacked and slashed their way along. A few large snakes had been slain along the way, just as a precaution.

"It's blasted hot in here," Ralf said in a disagreeable voice. "And the air stinks." He was not used to feeling so confined. The jungle weighed down on them all. The massive tree canopies hung with creepers and stringy moss overhead made it hard to get more than an occasional peek at the sky. The lush and exuberant undergrowth gave it an oppressive, claustrophobic feeling. You could not see more than a few feet ahead in any direction. Even Haroun, the ambitious lad who had begged to go with them, drooped.

"We'll take a break then," Sinbad said, wiping his brow below his turban. There was a group of rocks around a small pool where the men could sit back and rest. "Do not drink that," he warned Samad, who bent to scoop water to his lips. "It is generally filled with liver worms. Stick with the waterskins we brought with us!"

"But… but I drank mine already!" he complained.

"Then you are a greedy fool, Samad," the other man with them said darkly. "Pray to Allah that we find something fresher than this cesspit to sip from."

"I will die in this heat with no water!" Samad was beginning to sound irrational.

"I will give you a sip of mine, but you get no more than that. We will find clean water soon enough," Sinbad reassured him. The man greedily accepted the skin and began to gulp it down.

"That's enough!" Ralf said, grabbing it away and shoving him roughly. "Go sit down!"

"But I am still very thirsty!" Samad complained. He squatted for a few minutes but watched them all with mistrust. Suddenly he sprang to his feet. "That boy should give me his water; he does not need as much as a man!" He stomped over to Haroun with the idea of wrestling the skin from him. Sinbad and Ralf both started to rise up and he stopped in his tracks.

"Touch him and you'll need water no more," Sinbad warned him, his hand on his scimitar's hilt.

Samad looked around him uneasily with wild eyes, and then he ran off.

"Good riddance," said the other man, and he closed his eyes with his hands behind his head. Haroun looked from one to the other, confused.

"We shouldn't separate," Ralf said as he glanced around him suspiciously. "We don't know what's in here."

"A man can die in this heat without water," Sinbad said quietly. "He is likely already delirious. Go bring him back then if you are so worried, my friend. Just be careful."

"Always," said Ralf with a sigh, heaving his great bulk to his feet. He didn't get three steps away before they heard a gurgling scream from Samad.

"Holy Odin, what now?" Ralf said as he charged off in the direction it came from, his big axe in his hands and murder in his cold blue eyes. Sinbad was beside him in an instant, his scimitar unsheathed, following the hastily hacked and trampled trail of their crewman. Haroun and the other man ran somewhat behind.

Ralf and Sinbad pulled up short, for what had captured Samad was something out of a nightmare to behold. He had ventured to pick what he thought was a luscious red fruit from the smooth, swollen gray trunk of a huge tree with long, thin, bluish green tube like branches without leaves or needles. As soon as it sensed him close enough, long tentacles had shot out of those tubes and wrapped him securely, lifting him off his feet while he thrashed and cried out in terror. Slowly but inexorably tightening its grip, ribs and other bones were cracked, lungs were crushed, and blood poured from the unfortunate man's eyes, nose, and ears. With tremendous force it strangled the life from Samad until he flopped limp as a bundle of rags. Then the tentacles wrapped around his body lifted him high in the air, and slowly lowered him over a wet and vibrating gaping maw in the center crown of the thing.

Ralf snarled and swung his axe overhead. He made as if to charge in, but Sinbad held him back.

"Come to your senses my friend. We are too late, and he's dead already. You cannot save him now."

"I can't just stand here and let it eat him, Sinbad!" the red faced and angry Viking snapped, his muscles straining against the similarly corded brown arm thrown across his chest.

"There is no point, so I am ordering you to desist, Ralf," Sinbad said wisely, as they watched, horrified while the gigantic creature began to stuff the limp body of the unfortunate man into its ever-widening gullet through the mouth opening, the digestive juices of the thing bubbling up to liquefy skin and flesh. Great rings of muscular contractions beneath the epidermis of its trunk began to draw his corpse down inside. "This is a huge beast that could easily feast on every last one of us, and not something we can make much headway against. Samad doomed himself when he ran off from our party. We should go past it now while it's occupied."

Sickened beyond all words, the men made their way back to the waterhole. Gathering their things, they took leave of that area, going well around the tentacle-tree beast. Soon they were back to hacking and slashing their way through the last of the jungle, each one hyper alert, and wondering what other kinds of horror waited for them next.

Of the three men, only Henri had any battlefield experience. But what stood him in better stead were his younger years as a poacher in the forests belonging to nobles. There, no more than the snap of a twig or the whisper of a branch pulled aside might indicate the passage of game or an armed warden with orders to kill interlopers on sight. So when he heard the pattering of big feet, and looked back to see the bushes swaying, he called his companions to draw their weapons.

"To arms *mes amis*, something is stalking us, and there is more than one." His bow was already drawn with an arrow nocked and ready as he looked around wildly for a good place to make a stand. Whatever they were, the creatures were large and persistent. That marked them as predators and he and his companions prey.

Dropping the casks, the two men drew their swords. Looking behind them, they noted the height of the waving brush, and decided to run for it. They tore out of the forest fringe and diagonally across the beach. They headed back toward the boats, abandoning the foreign archer to his fate.

The leading man was not more than a few yards away when a lumbering body broke out of the jungle fringe to shuffle rapidly after him. It was a lizard the size of a pony, mottled dark in greens with black stripes; its color gradually changing to the pattern of the sand around it as it patiently ran the man down. A long yellow tongue with a forked tip lashed out and tasted the air, and then its mouth opened wide. Long strings of thick saliva ran over its many sharp teeth to drip to the sand below as it came shuffling on.

The man kept running, screaming for help, when another lizard darted out in front of him to cut off his escape. The second one lunged forward and his blade cut into its face, making it recoil and screech in pain. By then the first one had him by a leg, and he felt its teeth sinking to the bone as it hamstrung him. He went down with cries of agonized terror as it clamped down and tore chunks of flesh from his calf and thigh, the spurting blood quickly turning the light sand dark.

The second man had headed for the water, deciding to take his chances in the current. One more lizard followed him and he stood at bay before the lapping waves as it marched on, unfazed by the idea of having to wade in after him. He raised his sword in defiance and then dove under, the lizard only following up to the point where it stood belly deep. There were other creatures in the tide who hunted more efficiently than it did, and so it turned back and began stalking over to where one of its companions was tearing away at a severed limb while the half dead man laid moaning, writhing, and bleeding out his last on a lonely stretch of beach.

Henri had his own pursuers. He was shaking with fright, but his battle senses were better honed than those two simple sailors. He had let loose a couple of quick shots that took the foremost creature racing at him in the throat, dropping it quickly before he ran for his life. He knew he could not out distance the three others who were chasing him over the long haul, so as he sprinted, he angled his escape toward a place where he at least had hopes of making a stand. A group of three palms spaced closely together, the smallest one leaning out toward the open water, afforded him a chance to get off the ground. His bow over his shoulders, he quickly leapt to the trunk of the bent over palm, and feeling it flexing under his weight, catapulted to the next one, which he shinnied up. Where the curve of them came closest together, he braced himself between each ridged surface and brought his bow around.

"Now you die, foul ones," he said as he sighted carefully and let loose, hearing a satisfying thump and answering squeal as an arrow hit home. One of the big beasts went down thrashing, an arrow embedded deeply in an eye. Two more came over and began feasting on their companion before it even stopped twitching.

"*Mon Dieu*, you are the *féroces cannibales!*" he said as he nocked and readied another arrow and let it fly, that one hitting home as well. The last one took two arrows to dispatch with. "The world will be a better place without any of your kind in it." He was so busy picking his shots and trying to hit the big creatures swarming the beach, he had forgotten all about the one who had chased the man into the waves.

A light scraping of the wet sand below and behind him was his only warning. He leapt away just in time, for the small palm bowed under the weight of the beast that had stalked him up into the trees. It had lunged at him, just missing catching his boot in its teeth. It stood just above him on the now horizontal trunk that sagged beneath its weight, looking down and hissing. That long yellow tongue ran out. It was obviously confused that this prey had not gotten up to run off.

Henri knew that once he moved, he was likely a dead man. His bow was trapped beneath his body, dug into the sand. He had a belt knife drawn and an arrow in his other hand.

So it is just between you and moi, foul one. Dieu veuillez être miséricordieux! But if I die here, may it be as un personne qui a commis un acte courageux! Let them say Henri Delacroix was a man among men!

With a wild yell he sprang up and went over backwards. As the creature dropped heavily after him, he was back down on one knee, his bow was in his hands, and an arrow nocked. He let fly at point blank range. Just as the jaws lunged forward to snap on him, that arrow imbedded itself in the creature's mouth and up into the brain cage.

Slowly, the light in the eyes dimmed, the pupils contracted to mere slits. The large beast clacked its jaw and gave a shudder before it fell heavily sideways and lay unmoving in the sand, mere inches away.

Henri would never tell anyone later why his britches were soggy. Only he knew that he had actually wet himself in those last tense moments. He waded into the lapping surf, and let the salt water wash away all evidence of his personal embarrassment. On the beach behind him lay one man's mangled corpse and those of seven great beasts, already being picked at by scavenging gulls. Their bones would join many in making new dunes when the monsoon season storms pushed the water level high.

He gathered up the single water cask he could find, and headed back to where they left the landing boats, wary at every step for new dangers.

Tishimi had set aside her weapons. She sat alone in a lotus position on the aft deck, looking out over the water but seeing nothing. She was deep in meditation, trying to clear her mind and heart of all angry, unpleasant feelings.

Omar watched her a while before he approached. The female warrior was someone he seldom spoke to, for he did not approve of women being in places where only men were normally allowed. But Sinbad thought highly of her, and often took her advice, and he had nowhere to turn with the captain gone ashore.

"Begging pardon for disturbing you, Mistress Tishimi, but I need your counsel," he said in a low voice.

"It is no matter, Omar," she replied in a quiet tone as she gracefully unfolded her legs from that impossible arrangement, and stood to face him. "What may I do to assist you?" she asked with a bow, before picking up her weapons and tying them back to her belt.

He looked uncomfortable. "Those men injured in the last battle... one of them is shaking now and his swollen belly is twisting like a camel about to give birth. When my fifth wife had twin sons, she looked so, though not that thin and pale. I ask your opinion about what we can do for him."

"I will come with you," she said, slipping into her sandals and padding behind him. She still had a noticeable limp, though not as pronounced as earlier in the day. The rest and some gentle stretching had done her good, for all she had fretted about being left behind.

Below in the semi-darkness, as they passed through the crew hold to the storage area beyond that functioned as a sickroom, many pairs of eyes glared at her for violating their sanctum. Tishimi ignored them, focusing on the problem at hand. "How bad are they?" she asked.

"I am surprised any of them still live. They barely cling to life; yet inside, it seems as if some part of them lives on. Their bodies are bloated and lumpy, and the stomach moves of its own accord." He picked up a candle in a holder and led her inside the smaller hold.

Even normally unflappable Tishimi had to draw in a quick breath at the sight of the four men. Scarcely breathing and eyes wide open, the four skeletal figures stared at nothing. Yet each one had a huge rounded gut with shapes that wiggled and squirmed beneath the overstretched skin, and now two of them were trembling violently. As she watched, the mouth of the first one fell open and he spasmed upwards, his spine arching with audible cracking noises.

Omar drew in a breath and whispered, "Allah be merciful, this is not normal!"

Tishimi had to agree. "I fear a parasite. Get the others out of here, and latch the door securely behind me. What I must do is not for all eyes to see. You have to trust me, please."

"I do," Omar said as she drew her swords. The parchment-like epidermis over the first man's bulging midsection began to split open and many curved tailed things with wings began to tumble out. They were similar to the demons that came with the storm, only smaller and without limbs, though they had wings, a long curled body with ridges like a grub, bulging eyes and sucking mouth. They were wet and sticky and they vibrated their wings to dry, making a buzzing, rattling sound that was reminiscent of large bees.

"Go now, Omar; send your crewman on deck! I will handle this. Captain Sinbad's orders," Tishimi added harshly.

Against his better judgment as a Sindh man, he set down the candle and left, securing well the door behind him. She barred herself in with a small chest and a barrel for good measure. As the first of the small flying things began to lift off the man's dead body, her blades came up and crossed, and Tishimi took a battle stance. She began to swing and whir as a pestilence flock of the old world came streaming at her, their mouths open with newborn hunger for fresh blood.

Furious was the onslaught, and just as menacing was the response. Tishimi Osara's mind went to that quiet place where all deadly warriors go as their instincts take over in a battle. Her face set in a grimace of defiance; she put all her training, and every ounce of her long restrained anger and frustration at being a female warrior in a man's world, into her craft. Light on her feet, she leapt and danced a macabre ballet of flashing blades that left nothing alive in its wake. She swung the twin swords in endless arcs and curves, cutting through small bodies with precision and accuracy that only a master of the martial arts would be able to achieve.

Within minutes two thirds of her attackers had been hacked to pieces and the second body was just beginning to rupture. She never paused long enough to catch her breath but continued her blinding assault. Back and forth, up and down, in diagonal lines and great swoops, her lightning blades cut through the press, not allowing a single small body to survive. Tishimi was in her element, and the floor and walls of the storage area were soon splattered with the remains of the infant sea djinn. She stood ankle deep in their oozing remains.

The third body was just splitting open as she finished with the second group. She bled from scratches and nips in several places, but none of them had managed to bear her down. Whatever it was that the demons did to implant their evil seed had happened to men who went prostrate beneath them. Tishimi was determined to stay on her feet.

When every last member of the first three broods was dead or dying, she took one moment to compose herself. What she must do now, no man aboard that ship could know, for it violated every tenet of their faith as well as her own. The last body still did not show immediate signs of bursting open, though the abdominal skin heaved and bulged with the teaming life within. This had been a big man, with much muscle and fat reserves and his belly was now the size of the huge Egyptian melons that they sometimes took on as payment for cargo. He did not see her or recognize his surroundings. He would not survive the day.

Blades crossed before her face, she said, "I am the sword and the sword is neither right nor wrong. I am the warrior and the warrior fights with honor and truth." Her hands swept apart, went up and came down, slicing into the body that quaked and heaved before her.

There was no blood, just an erupting ooze of grey green fluid as five very large and nearly fully formed djinn spewed forth. These were not the small larvae of the other two bodies but almost adult size with grasping limbs, very angry and hungry. They did not wait for their wings to dry but sprang directly at her with snarling maws agape, claws and fangs bared.

Tishimi backpedaled to give herself room and that is where her sore leg betrayed her. Weakened and stiffened by the endless activity and so little rest, it slipped in the gore beneath her sandals and twisted. She lost her balance and went down with her blades only between her and the vicious, angry djinn that were trying to fasten their teeth in her and inject the venom that would make her catatonic and unable to fight them off. Then she would be come a host body for their next brood, lying drained and hovering near death until conditions were right for them to burst forth.

As she fought to regain her footing, one of them got past her blade and fastened its teeth in her left shoulder for a moment. She rolled and crushed it, but not before some of the venom was absorbed. An ice cold sensation was followed by spreading numbness as her well-trained mind fought to control her slow responding limbs. The affected arm drooped to her side and the wakizashi dropped from nerveless fingers.

The other four swarmed her. She batted them off with the Katana, heaving herself drunkenly to her feet. Her eyes were swimming and it was hard to stay focused, her legs felt like jellyfish drifting, but she was a fighter.

"My father's blood has tempered this blade. I cannot die," she said as she assumed a two-handed hold that would give her the strength and dexterity she needed. "My enemies fall before me, as the song of the ancients rings in my ears." She felt a bit stronger and the blade began to cut slow arcs around her, though she was still clumsy with the light-headedness, the sore leg, and numb arm.

"I am one with my sword; there is no beginning to me, no end to it. I

I am one with my sword...

fight…" she sliced the air with greater control, "for what is…" she was able to move forward with more assurance, "sacred and just!"

Tishimi lunged forward, and while her legs shook, they held her, and some feeling was returning to her hand. She scored a hit on another one of the creatures and it backed off squealing. "I have no fear, for I am the avenger of all that is right!" A cut just missed as the creature dodged, but at least it feared her enough to move away. "This foulness shall not pass me by, for I live to serve," she followed the first swing with a back cut with the tip of the katana that sliced it in half, and then targeted another, "the Higher Ones. Oh hear me, Marisha-Tan, goddess of the samurai!" She scored another hit and her vision was clearing as she jabbed it and the creature went down. "I protect my friends and my honor with your dedicated blade."

One left, and it was dodging her.

"Let nothing pass my blade; that I might someday avenge my father's death, and die in old age with dignity!"

Her voice rose into a triumphant war cry and the blood rose in her pale cheeks as Tishimi became a blurred maelstrom of fury. She swung and sliced, leapt and lunged, dancing on lively feet that scarcely felt the floor; they were down for so few seconds. She chased that last creature of death all over the small enclosed room, seemingly tireless, infused with the power of a heartfelt prayer. And perhaps her patron goddess heard her, locked in a storeroom within a ship on a sea far from home, for eventually the creature made a fatal mistake.

Mad with hunger, the last of its brood still alive, it came right at her. She stood her ground and cut it in thirds, and all three pieces fell to the gory floor.

Not a smile passed her thin lips, not a bit of weariness rounded her shoulders. She held her Katana before her face, the blade upright between her eyes. "Thank you Marisha-Tan, for your blessing. Thank you father for your wisdom, and your sacrifice. I have done well because of you both."

She bent and picked up her wakizashi, and wiped both blades on the clothing of one of the dead men. Then sheathing her blades, she began to move the barrel and the chest, as Omar and other voices called from the other side.

When the door opened, Tishimi Osara, covered in blood, sweat, and the ooze of dead djinn, stood alone and triumphant in a room full of carnage. "It is safe now, they are all dead," she said quietly, walking past the stunned mate of the Blue Nymph and the gaping crewmen. "I apologize for the deaths of your companions, for that could not be helped. I am also sorry for the mess. Right now, I desire a quiet place to bathe and then some rest."

"We will see to this," Omar said in a hushed tone. As she walked away through the crew's quarters, he began to issue orders to the men, not one of which ever questioned why the only woman aboard should be given such privileges. From that day forward, there was not a man on the Blue Nymph who did not have great respect for the aloof and lonely female samurai.

✿ ✿ ✿

The cliffs were sharp and sheer; seemingly the only path was straight up. The last man deserted them sometime at the base, for he had a great fear of falling to his death. Sinbad let him go; if he survived they would deal with him later.

This was where the boy Haroun came in handy. He was agile and used to such terrain. The plan was he would climb ahead and secure a line and they would then follow him up to a safe ledge until he scouted out a continuing route.

"In the Spin Ghar Mountains, where I am from, we know there is always a way to scale the rocks. The donkeys, goats, and wild things manage, so we follow them. There will be game trails here, and with no snow, I will easily find them," Haroun bragged as he checked the heavy rope bound around his waist and then began his climb. Surefooted as one of those goats, he found hand and footholds that Sinbad and Ralf would never have seen. Eventually he located the first safe spot, a projecting jut of rock, and tied off the rope.

"Come on!" he called down. "One of you big men at a time. It is safe!"

"If we fall, we go to our deaths," Ralf rumbled with distaste.

"Think positively my friend," Sinbad said to him as he started hauling himself up the rope with his scimitar in its back scabbard and his offering sack tied around his neck. "There are treasures to be won!"

"There are always treasures," Ralf said with a sigh. "Too bad they cost so much to find!"

"Where's your sense of adventure?" Sinbad called back down as he eagerly climbed up the cliff as if he had not been trekking through a jungle all day. He was soon safe above and urging the Norseman on.

"I left mine in my other boots," Ralf grumbled as he hauled himself up the rope. "I am beginning to think that the endless raiding and plundering of my clan was a lot more profitable than this constant seafaring in search of new places to get killed."

"You can always return to that," Sinbad said sarcastically as he leaned over the edge and offered a strong and welcoming arm to grab.

"When I've made my fortune and have seen all the world," was the answer he got. Sinbad clapped him on the back. They were two of one spirit when it came to satisfying that burning urge to discover the secrets of new lands.

And so it went until well into the evening, where the sturdy lad would climb up ahead of them, and then toss the rope down. The wind blew harder as they got farther up, and a few times someone slipped and dangled helplessly until he could get his feet back under him. Eventually though, they only had one last long climb before the precipice was reached. Haroun made it up easily over the projecting ledge and then ran off. He came back in a few minutes, and threw the rope down. It didn't quite reach to where Sinbad and Ralf stood.

"There was nothing close by to tie it on. I had to find something a ways back. I am sorry, but you will have to climb a bit without the rope. I did my best, Captain!" he called down in an anxious voice.

"You did well today Haroun, don't be sorry," Sinbad said, beginning his climb. "No apologies needed."

Sinbad went first and other than a small piece of stone that crumbled beneath one grasping hand, he had no problem reaching the end of the rope. A lifelong sailor on ships with rigging that had to be climbed to trim sails; he was athletic and agile for a big man. Hand over hand he hauled himself up, until he could grip the rope between legs long callused from such climbs. He was soon at the top and looking down, he called out to Ralf, "Come my friend, we are at the highest point now! It will be easier once you are on top, the land here is grassy and flat."

"I'm coming," Ralf said without enthusiasm and he began to cautiously haul himself up the cliff side. He had the advantage of extra height and longer arms, which meant he would reach the end of the rope sooner. But unlike Sinbad, he had never done much climbing and he did not have an instinct for it. His weight was also against him.

He was almost within reach of the rope when the embedded rock he made the mistake of placing both booted feet on began to tilt and slip.

"Be careful!" Haroun shouted down. "That rock is not part of the cliff!" Sinbad's worried face appeared over the edge beside him.

"Just a few more inches Ralf—you can make it!"

Breathing hard, Ralf scrambled to find another foothold, while his fingers dug into the rock crevices above him like claws. His left foot still on the original rock, the right was precariously wedged into a cleft only large enough to accept his toes.

"I don't dare move," Ralf said between gritted teeth. "I have no place to go but down!"

"Lay against the cliff, it will lighten your weight," Haroun suggested. "Then there is a knob to your right that will give you a safe handhold. Move your fingers over there."

As Ralf shifted, the rock beneath his left foot finally let go. Spinning beneath his boot, it dropped and went rebounding down the cliff wall to land with a muffled thud into the jungle below. He almost panicked then and lost his footing altogether. If not for the corded strength of his mighty arms, he would have fallen to his death. As it was he lay flat against the rock face, almost spread eagle, and trembling with the strain of trying to hang on.

"Don't move, I'm coming down for you," Sinbad said as he divested himself of sword and sack and began to shinny back down toward where Ralf was.

"You can't help me up, Sinbad; I weigh more than you do!"

"Never tell me what I can or can't do, Norseman," Sinbad growled from between gritted teeth as he reached the end of the rope. "Give me your hand," he insisted, gripping the rope with palm, fingers, and ankles wrapped around it and leaning down as far as he could.

"Sinbad… be reasonable! I will pull you to your death!" Ralf warned him.

"Take my hand Ralf, and that is an order!" Sinbad thundered in that voice that could fill a room.

"All right, don't shout the cliff down over my head," the Viking retorted as he let go with his left hand and clasped Sinbad's muscular brown forearm. The gesture was returned and the two men clamped onto each other. Sinbad flexed every muscle in his back and shoulders. He grunted and heaved with all his might. A fraction of an inch at a time he hauled the Viking, who weighed far more than he did, upwards. He strained so hard to hold on, his muscles burned and tore loose, but his grip was solid and he would not let go.

Encouraged that he was not going to fall to his death after all, Ralf began to slowly walk his way up toward where he could reach the end of the rope. He grasped it with his free hand. "I have it, Sinbad!" he said joyfully.

"Thank Allah for that," Sinbad said with a grimace of discomfort. He turned himself upward and began to rapidly climb back up to the top.

"Hurry Captain, the weight is too much! The knot is slipping and I can barely hold it in place," Haroun called anxiously from where he was squatting with the tail end of the piece in his hands, struggling to keep it from slipping over the rock it was tied to.

"I've got it, boy!" Sinbad said with a jaunty smile as he came bounding over the edge. He soon stood between the rock and the drop off, hauling on the line to bring Ralf up. When the Viking's head broke over the cliff, Haroun gave a cheer and clapped his hands. Ralf heaved himself up and over, and rolled onto the grass, panting and smiling. Sinbad flopped down next to him and they both laughed like idiots, as the adrenaline fueled heroics faded into sheer relief.

"It is a fine day to be alive," the Viking said in his characteristic rumble tinged with mirth.

"They all are, Ralf," Sinbad answered with a flashing smile. "They all are."

❊ ❊ ❊

The sun was going down as the three adventurers approached the huge stone temple with trepidation. They were expecting another trap, or that some monster would jump out at them. It was far later in the day than Sinbad had hoped it would be when he set out at dawn.

As they entered the area within the great columns, it was dark as night inside, so they could not see the amber eyes that studied them intently.

"It has to be here somewhere," Sinbad said in a low voice that sounded vexed. He had his sword drawn, for the creepy sensation of being watched had caused the fine hairs on the back of his neck to rise.

"What makes you so sure?" Ralf rumbled his axe already loose in his hands. The boy Haroun, the rope wrapped around his waist and Sinbad's sack over his shoulder, brought up the rear. He looked around nervously and swallowed a few times.

"I just know," Sinbad answered uneasily as he stepped forward. "You get a sixth sense for these things–"

Suddenly, hundreds of candles in the temple flared of their own accord. Sinbad and Ralf took a step backward, momentarily blinded. When their eyes adjusted, a massive multicolored iridescent beast stood in the center of pillars of stone studded with crystals and mica that twinkled as they reflected the light. The great head inclined downward and amber eyes that seemed at once both kindly and wary watched them curiously.

"Welcome Sinbad El Ari; and you as well Ralf, son of Gunar, of the cold north seas. You have done well to get this far. You are both a distance from home, though I believe the Norseman has traveled the farthest. I see you have brought a brave young Pashtun named after a Caliph with you. I am sure he has proved quite useful." Its eyes took in all three of them as it turned its head first this way, and then that.

Ralf gripped his axe tighter and watched it with his characteristic ice blue glare. The beast was a colorful and interesting mix of bird and mammal and obviously intelligent, but it was immense and the talons appeared to be formidable. He was very uneasy that it seemed to know who he was. Haroun shrank back and made himself as small as possible, ready to flee at a moment's notice if things got ugly. Sinbad seemed to be the only one who was not the least bit bewildered by its presence.

"Hail wise and mighty Simurgh, I have come over ocean and land, fighting storms and attacks by monsters and demons, just to ask you a few questions," he began.

The huge creature smiled, showing many long, sharp teeth. "The danger of your journey is regrettable, Sinbad, but a necessary consequence of the search for such knowledge. Mankind, I find, must be tempered and proven; and great men of any age must be challenged even harder. I know what you seek, and it is not something to be trifled with.

"In later eras," it cocked its head, as if thinking seriously, and the back and neck feathers ruffled in a wave of dizzying color, "such men will go to seek new worlds amongst the stars. In this age, there is still much about this world that is unknown. Not all these places you will go are worth seeing, Sinbad, and most are very dangerous. You are the son of a prince and a princess; you should have enough wealth and power for ten such men. Are you sure this is what you want?

"Be honest about your intentions," the Simurgh warned with a predatory look. "I do not have to grant you anything, and you will not fool me with pretty words and subterfuge. I can see all the paths your life might take. Do not think I cannot understand a lie, even from honeyed lips such as yours."

Sinbad shook his head and his now dirty and disheveled turban almost came free. "I would not insult your intelligence so. I am positive this is what I want," he said without hesitation. "Oh, certainly I expect to find treasures, but that is only so I can fund more voyages. It is my life's calling to go to sea and explore our world. I cannot rest while there are undiscovered lands waiting for me." It was the most honest thing he had ever told anyone.

The Simurgh looked pleased and its ruffled head feathers lay flat as it nodded. "So it is not *only* about the treasure... very good. Now let us see what you have brought to me."

Sinbad motioned for Haroun to hand him the sack. He undid the ties and opened it, pulling out a packet of gold and silver coins, a cloth wrapped around a long string of large and perfect pearls, and many different gems. Ralf looked on with amazement but Haroun's eyes nearly popped from his head. He had never seen such riches!

"I see you have been quite successful," the Simurgh said as it craned its neck to examine the small fortune laid before it on the fitted stone block floor. "Seemingly you could retire from seafaring and live comfortably for some years on this alone. Yet I have no use for such wealth here. My needs are not that of men, Sinbad. Try again."

Sinbad sighed, for while he had not expected the treasure to be enough on its own, he had hoped to at least pay part of his debt with it. He reached back in the sack and pulled out and ancient scroll on wooden rollers tied with silk cord. He undid the knots and unfurled it.

"This is an eyewitness accounting of the birth of civilization. I found it in a cave in the middle of the desert. I've been offered a king's ransom for it several times, and someone sent assassins against me to steal it the day I had it appraised in Baghdad."

"Which is where you met the female samurai; yes, I recall," the Simurgh said with a toothy smile. It peered down at the scroll. "This is interesting material, but I lived through that age, so I have no need to read about it— besides, it contains some inaccuracies. You should sell it and buy more boats."

"Sounds like a good idea," Ralf interjected but grew silent when Sinbad glared and the Simurgh eyed him warily. "I mean, more ships gives us more treasure we can haul," he added with a shrug.

The Simurgh's head went back and it wheezed a rusty sounding laugh. "The Norseman has an uncomplicated outlook, but it is refreshingly honest. I can see why you enjoy his companionship."

"Yes, he's certainly rather simple at times. What about this?" Sinbad said and pulled forth a short but wide and heavy gold chalice with a flourish. "It is precious in its own right, but is rumored to have caught the blood of a prophet who was ordered slain by an enemy general."

The Simurgh's eyes lit up at that, and it nestled down to squint and study the piece before speaking. "This is a genuine artifact whose very rumor will fuel a holy war. Armed zealots with banners of glory will come from all over the world to find it. I do not believe we should leave that laying around. I will keep it here, and we're not to speak of it again. However, it is still not enough to trade for what you ask of me, Sinbad El Ari…"

Sinbad's patience had worn thin. "What else do you require of me?" he said irritably, turning the sack inside out to show it was empty. "I have offered you all I can spare! I still must pay my crew and my companions, one of which waits for us down on the beach, likely thinking we are already dead," he added in a more subdued tone, thinking of the setting sun. "I have lost several good men and endangered many others to get here, just to find out that whatever I give you is never going to be enough." He sat back on his heels with his muscular brown arms held wide, and a disgusted look on his face.

"Perhaps this is because you do not value anything that you offer me," the Simurgh said quietly, as it nestled down before him. "You do have something on you that you treasure highly, and yet you refuse to part with it. You could offer me that."

Sinbad sprung to his feet and began to pace back and forth. "What? My life? My ship? My right arm? Or perhaps my sword? What good would that do me, if I can no longer sail or fight! Bah—I am tired of riddles! I might as well leave while I can, and go back to carrying merchandise and chasing rumors."

He bent to scoop up his things and the Simurgh shot out a talon toward him. Haroun gasped and nervously jumped backwards, though the boy drew his knife to defend his captain anyway. Ralf's axe was in his hands and swinging overhead when the Simurgh stopped him with a look.

"This, I will accept as an offering," it said, as a single huge claw pulled on a thong from around Sinbad's neck. On the end of it was an amulet stone carved with a fully maned lion of inset silver, the eye a tiny but flawless sapphire. The setting was gold, with a bar through it from which it hung.

Sinbad was aghast. "It is not very expensive, but has great sentimental value to me. It was my father's; my mother had it made for him as part of her dowry. He gave it to me when I became a man. It is all I have left of him. But if that is what it takes…" he lifted the thong off his neck slowly, and hung it on the talon before him, and then closed it up over the amulet. "Take it."

The Simurgh smiled and held the amulet up for the others to see. "Behold, Sinbad El Ari gives from his heart. And so I shall do the same. Your companions will be waiting elsewhere for you Sinbad, but you and I must talk alone this night, for what I will say and do are for your eyes and ears only."

It raised its head and called out in a strange, liquid tone. A pair of huge birds flew over the cliff on quiet wings, taking Ralf and Haroun up by their shoulders in their claws. Sinbad leapt to his feet at the first hint of trouble, his scimitar drawn. The Simurgh put out a warning talon to restrain him.

"Do not fear. These servants of mine will not harm any of you." It spoke to each of the birds in their own language of screeches and squawks, and they flew off with their burdens. Haroun had fainted and he hung limp and silent in the grasping claws of his escort but they could hear Ralf shouting and cursing for a very long time.

"Where are they going?" Sinbad asked with alarm as he watched them disappear in the darkening sky.

"To the beach, where your other bold companion awaits," the Simurgh answered with a smile that was less fierce and somehow more seductive. It dropped Sinbad's amulet back at his feet. "Keep that, for now you must give me what I truly desire," it said in a sultry voice. Its form shimmered and contracted; until it became a very beautiful and desirable dark haired, bronze skinned young woman clad in nothing more than translucent rainbow veils. The sight of her was very arousing.

"You... are a goddess?" Sinbad asked with an indrawn breath.

"I am, at times known as Isis," the Simurgh answered as she lowered long, dark lashes demurely and sidled forth into his warm and waiting grasp. "And I desire many children to raise and send forth in this age. Do you understand what price I want from you now Sinbad?" Her slender arms went up around his neck as her curvaceous body melded into his muscular one.

"I think I can guess," he said with a smile as he bent his head down and his blue eyes met her melting amber gaze. Dark lips sought ruby red softness, as all but one candle went out with a whoosh.

✿ ✿ ✿

"We need to go back and find him!" Ralf said darkly as dawn broke over the ocean and streamers of light played over the water, illuminating the beach. The Viking had fallen into a sound slumber as soon as he hit the sand, but the first light had awakened him. Haroun was still asleep beneath the boat he had crawled under, exhausted from his labors the day before. "Shake the boy; we'll need him for climbing the cliff."

"I tell you, it's going to be fine, those big birds were most gentle with you. Sit down; have something to eat," Henri said as he poked at the driftwood fire and then handed his large and agitated companion a stick with a long strip of charred meat.

"How can you stand this stuff?" Ralf said with distaste as he looked it over and tried not to recall that it was cut off the body of a giant lizard before he bit into it. "Smells nasty and it's tough," he said around a mouthful.

"Tastes very much like *poulet* to me—perhaps a trifle gamier." Henri grabbed one for himself, blowing on it before ripping off a few shreds, and smacking his lips. "You'll get used to it."

"I don't intend to be here that long," Ralf said around a chewy mouthful that he almost choked on as Sinbad himself came jauntily strolling along the dawn beach, whistling a sea chantey. He waved and began running toward them, and they trotted out to greet him, even Haroun sitting up to grind the sleep out of his eyes and stretch. Ralf reached Sinbad first and banged him on the back hard enough to knock the wind out of him.

"Capitaine, you are looking fine, most happy!" Henri greeted him. "Does this mean you have obtained the formula we sought?"

"Yes I did!" Sinbad said with a mischievous smile, and his blue eyes had a smoky and satisfied glint. He pulled a small square of parchment with ink marks on it from his shirt and waved it under their noses. "Everything is here, listed in order, and while we will have to do some searching and careful trading, we should be able to assemble this easily enough. The biggest problem is finding the right binder to put it together, because it must be mounted on the ship and has to resist wind, salt, and weather."

"Omar might have some idea," Ralf said as they headed for the boats. Henri bobbed along beside them, taking two steps for every one of his longer legged companions.

"You look like a man who has spent his night alone in a bordello. Have you eaten? I have some very fine meat here–"

"I'm fine," Sinbad said, cutting Henri off. "While the tide is out, let's get back to the ship and be on our way. We have much to be grateful for my friends, and planning to do."

❈ ❈ ❈

As the one boat they decided to take with them was poled and paddled back through the reefs to the waiting Blue Nymph, a small and solitary veiled figure watched them go with amber eyes that had turned mournful. As they reached their vessel and the order was given to cast off, long bronze fingers went to ruby red lips. She blew a kiss, starting a breeze to blowing. It became a wind that ruffled her rainbow iridescent veils and luxurious obsidian hair. It carried over the water, filling the indigo sails that helped pull a proud ship back out to sea. She watched as they disappeared over the horizon, her hands cradling her abdomen as a sly smile played on her face. And then she turned and walked back into the dark temple, and was seen no more.

THE END

Sinbad and Me

When the call went out from Airship 27 for a new Sinbad series, I was thrilled! I have loved the old swashbuckling, seafaring movies since I was a kid in the 60s and 70s, watching them on my family's black and white TV. I've always been captivated by Ray Harryhausen's stop motion animation, and it's fueled more than one story idea for me over the years—for even in this age of green screen sets with CGI monsters, it holds up extremely well. To be able to participate in a writing project with that same Saturday afternoon cinematic appeal, as well as a motley cast of regular characters that I could easily picture, got the juices flowing immediately. I popped out a quick idea based on a mythical creature of ancient Persia as well as the quest for a formula to make a magical navigation device and I was off and racing to the keyboard.

I am primarily a fantasy fiction writer; though I have taken forays into other genres; so Sinbad and his world have always been very near and dear to my heart. Most of what I write is my original material, and I have plenty of it, so for someone else's story world to captivate me like this did, it has to be very special. In my experience with writing, some stories start out well but bog down in the middle somewhere and others putter along from beginning to end, but now and then I will have a story that I just can't write fast enough. Happily this was one of the latter varieties, and because there were many other demands on my time while I was working on it, it was frustrating not to be able to sit down as often or as long as I wanted to and work at it.

Most stories don't turn out all that much like the original idea, but my feeling on finishing it is this one is far better than what I envisioned. Writing is always hard work, so I can't brag that it practically wrote itself, but it was one of the least torturous assignments I've been handed. I've always been a visual thinker when it comes to writing, and not only could I hear the characters, but I could see them, talk to them, and watch them going about their business. There were nights I fell asleep thinking about the next scene, and would wake up with an idea that just had to be jotted down. That's how you know when you're 'in the zone' with a project.

The hardest thing with writing about Sinbad was trying to find something he had not done before or monsters and menaces he hadn't faced. He has a long and interesting history from his appearances in the Arabian Nights tales through his many permutations on the silver screen and in various other media. I studied everything I could find trying to understand what had been done and overdone. He certainly had been shipwrecked a lot, and so I needed a reason for that—starting with a new crew was often a problem pirates and adventurers faced, as their reputation for getting into dangerous situations spread. One thing of course that stands out with our intrepid son of the seven seas is his lust to find and explore exotic new lands, which are often populated with unfriendly hordes and the creatures of myth and legend. That went into the story too. And since we were told up front to take very bold strokes with the adventure and danger, and this is New Pulp, which is high action writing, I let my imagination run wild. I'm particularly proud of my choice of monsters and their mayhem, because most of them are not stock creatures from the B movies. Along the way, there were some more natural dangers salted in, as well as the kind of battlefield camaraderie you see when people work together in harrowing circumstances for a common goal.

One of the strengths of this series is the multinational/multiracial core group that supports Sinbad. Fleshing out the characters of Omar the intrepid and cantankerous first mate, Ralf Gunarson the big and bold Viking, Henri Delacroix the rather smarmy Gaul archer, and Tishimi Osara the dedicated female samurai trying to fit into a male world, was actually a lot of fun. High Fantasy thrives on groups of specialists and I was happily in my element with them. As I went along my focus was often on the interplay of these supporting characters, who sometimes bicker and jest like family members, and their love and loyalty for their adventuresome captain and the restless seafaring life he has given them. They were very clearly drawn for me from the outset and by the end of the tale I felt I knew them all quite well. I had a lot of fun working with them, and really look forward to writing another one of these.

This was a great project and something I've very proud to have been involved with. I still recall the younger me, sitting glued to that TV screen, eating up every scene, dreaming of a day when I could write such a flamboyant and captivating story. Not everyone gets to work with a character they've loved for over 45 years. So here it is folks, my nod to the action-adventure works of the past, all gussied up and refitted. The decks are swept, the sail freshly dyed, and there's a bright new coat of paint drying on the wood. Soon the majestic Blue Nymph will leave port once more with her smiling captain at the tiller, whistling a sea chantey, when he's not shouting orders or swinging his scimitar and grinning from ear to ear.

Enjoy!

NANCY HANSEN - A writer of fantasy and adventure fiction for over 20 years, she is the author of both the novel FORTUNE'S PAWN, and TALES OF THE VAGABOND BARDS—the first anthology of her brand new imprint, Hansen's Way. Both books are available from Pro Se Press. Her short stories have been featured in many issues of Pro Se Presents and she is also Assistant Editor for the company. She currently resides in beautiful rural northeastern Connecticut with a very understanding and supportive family who don't mind missed meals and housework that doesn't get done while she wrestles with her muse.

SINBAD & the SAPPHIRE of the DJINN

by I.A. Watson

Sinbad ducked low, so the house-guard's scimitar shattered only a man-high wine jar. The sailor hooked the man's feet out from under him, sending him toppling down the staircase onto the other soldiers that followed after. To add to the confusion, Sinbad shouldered the other liquor containers down the steps too, toppling guards down into the courtyard beyond, setting the wine merchant screaming as his wares were wasted.

Sinbad sprinted along the balcony and leapt onto the roof. The varnished tiles were slippery but his bare feet found purchase enough to scramble to the apex. An arrow whirred past him. He made a deep elaborate bow at the archer before sliding down the other side and tumbling across to the adjacent flat roof.

"That way!" someone below shouted. "He's on the spice vendor's house!"

Sinbad grinned and leaped the ten feet onto the carpet-seller's mansion, and from there vaulted over to the jeweler's roof. He heard a yelp from behind as the first soldier to try and follow him misjudged the distance. He turned and saw the hapless guard clinging to the ledge above the precarious drop by one hand.

"You need to be more careful," the sailor warned the man as he hauled him back onto the balcony. A roundhouse left felled the guard before he could think of thanks or belligerence. "It's really not your day, is it?"

More arrows rattled across the distance between the buildings – and a pitchfork, for some reason. Sinbad waved at his pursuers and hauled the rope off a flagpole so he could loop it onto a crenulation of the next dwelling. By the time the soldiers had forced their way into the jeweler's house, the sailor was already hauling himself onto the tower of the armorer's guild.

Someone had been clever. A couple of guards were already waiting there for him.

Sinbad rolled, slid between the legs of the nearest soldier, and hauled hard at the man's sash. The guard spun round, dizzied. Sinbad claimed the red cloth and used it to leap onto the washing line between the armorer's roof and the courtesan house next door. He suspected it was a regular route.

"Sinbad!" one of the lovely young women in the compound below recognized him. She rose from her bathing pool to wave.

"Hello, ladies!" he called back as he balanced along the high wall around their seraglio. "I'm afraid I can't stop and chat just now. People trying to kill me."

"People are always trying to kill you," one perfumed beauty complained with a pout.

"What can I say? I have that kind of life!"

The sailor reached the far corner of the perimeter wall, from whence he could hook his way across to the silk merchant's apartment. That had a helpful decorative ridge running all the way around it and from there it was only one long jump onto the pan-tiles of the domed temple.

A trio of hopeful guards had come that way too, hoping to cut him off. Sinbad avoided a crude amateur spear-thrust and relieved the youngster of his weapon to fend off the fat older guard with the scimitar. It was easy to tangle both men with the polearm and leave them caught in the net in which they'd hoped to snare him.

That left only the archer. Sinbad downed the man with a precise belly-punch and borrowed his bow and quiver.

Sinbad fired arrows into the high palace wall twenty feet away from the temple's edge. The glazed blue bricks formed the newest part of the Caliph's fortress. Sinbad embedded a dozen shafts in what he hoped might be secure strongpoints between the stones, clenched the archer's twin belt knives in his teeth, and leaped for the distant wall.

The first arrow he caught snapped, and so did the second. For a moment it looked like the agile sailor would plunge down to the crowded marketplace below and end his adventures in a bone-shattering splat. But the third shaft held long enough for him to snatch a fourth and fifth. Before they too could splinter, Sinbad had the knives dug into the mortar between the blue bricks.

A shout from the temple roof warned him that the guards were up again. He was glad he'd removed the bow.

He began to climb, upwards and round the curve of the blue tower, out of sight of the men on the temple. He plunged the daggers into the gaps between stones, hoping that the cheap metal was sufficient to sustain his weight. Even his limber arms were beginning to ache when he reached the keyhole-shaped window beneath the topping minaret.

He climbed into a silk-swathed room and looked around.

A beautiful gauze-veiled woman noticed a man had just climbed into her boudoir. "Well now," she said, "This is unexpected."

Sinbad gave a courtly bow. "I apologies for the intrusion. I was just passing and decided to pay a visit."

The woman advanced boldly. She had oiled skin the color of creamed coffee and long raven hair filleted with pearls. Her yashmak was translucent, offering a glimpse of full red lips curved into an intrigued smile. "Did you forget something?" she suggested, gesturing to the sailor's current attire.

Sinbad was naked. His only clothing was a silver sapphire amulet around his neck.

"Alas, I had to leave my things behind when I needed to make a hasty departure," the sailor admitted. "I doubt the wine merchant will return them to me now. Shame, because I had that tunic from Byzantium."

"Do you know the penalty for intruding on a princess' bedchamber?" the woman enquired.

"Do I have to eat sherbet and drink a cup of cool wine with her while I tell her my story?" Sinbad ventured. He grinned a winning smile. "Why not let me tell you? As you see, I have nothing to hide."

The princess' own smile broadened. "Who are you?" she demanded. She examined the dark-skinned intruder carefully, noting his handsome, mischievous face, his tight-muscled body, his white-toothed smile, his confident pose.

"O fair moon of desire, they call me Sinbad the Sailor. I hope you might call me friend and darling. And what might I call you?"

"You are Sinbad? I have heard of a rogue and adventurer who sails on voyages of discovery and trade, then returns to Baghdad with fabulous riches only to squander them and vanish again in search of more."

"Squander is a strong word. Say rather that I have lots of friends who need my support. And I happen to like sailing strange seas and discovering things. I have a knack for it."

"Many in the city think you a liar, a mere pirate who loots other ships and spins fantastic stories of how he came by his wealth to hide his crimes."

Sinbad shook his head. "I never lie except when I need to. I might boast occasionally, but only to impress the fairest of ladies. Did I mention that my father was a Nubian prince and my mother a Moorish princess?"

The beautiful maiden decided that she wouldn't summon the guard yet. She tossed her visitor a linen burnoose to cover himself and poured him a goblet of chilled white wine. "I am Ayisha, a daughter of the Caliph of Baghdad. It is death for a man to speak with me alone."

"I'd better make the most of it, then," Sinbad grinned. "Why are you locked in a tower, beautiful Ayisha?"

"My father is dying. My suitors are persistent." She glanced at the window. "Not usually that persistent, I admit."

Sinbad sipped his drink, wrapped himself in his gown, and settled on the princess' bed. "If I were your suitor, no wall or tower would stay me from your side."

"I imagine not. So why are you here, Sinbad the Sailor?"

"Ah, you do want the story! Excellent. I love telling stories."

"I will hear your tale, in payment for your intrusion."

Sinbad shook his head. "I'm a merchant as well as a sailor, great lady. I know a bad bargain when I hear it. My stories are especially fine, guaranteed to enthrall and enchant, to make your heart pound and your skin tingle. They're worth far more than just the use of a convenient window."

"Are they now?" The princess tilted her head. "What are they worth, then?"

"Well, I think they deserve an attentive audience. Come and sit here on these cushions with me, dawn of all desire, where you can be comfortable as I talk. And if you think the tale worth it at the end, pay me the surplus in sweet kisses."

Ayisha raised one perfect painted eyebrow. "Does that work on ladies of your acquaintance?" she wondered.

"Almost always," Sinbad confessed. "Please don't spoil my average."

The princess glided over and folded her legs under her at the far edge of her bed. "Proceed, Sinbad the Sailor," she commanded.

Sinbad nodded and spoke: "Praise be to Allah, the beneficent king, creator of the universe, who set up the firmament without pillars and who stretched out the earth below. Know, O princess, that there was once a humble sailor who journeyed far from home and returned with fabulous treasures and wondrous companions. And lo, one day, once such companion spake unto Sinbad and said…"

"You must be the biggest idiot ever to stand on the decks of a ship!"

Sinbad looked hurt. "Maybe amongst the top ten," he admitted, "but hardly the absolute biggest, surely?"

"Shall we take a vote on it?" offered Omar, Sinbad's rough first mate, who had offered the opinion in the first place. "Henri?"

"Biggest," agreed the Gallic hunter.

"Ralf?"

The giant Viking was sweltering in the unfamiliar heat of the Al Basra docks and his temper was short. "Definitely," he confirmed.

"Rafi?"

The barber surgeon put down the razor he was stropping and nodded. "Yes, I think we have to say the biggest."

"Lady Tishimi?"

The strangest member of Sinbad's current crew was the remarkable young woman from the Isles of Nippon at the edge of the Endless Sea, a sword-maiden unlike any that had ever traveled as far as the lands of the Caliph Al-Haroun. She met Sinbad's gaze with fearless green eyes and pronounced her judgment. "A wise man does not make a wager he cannot win, nor gamble what he cannot afford to lose."

"Ah!" Sinbad exclaimed, holding up his index fingers to make a point, "That's where you're all making the mistake. You see, you're all thinking that the Blue Nymph can't make the journey to the Sapphire Isle faster than Anwar abd Anwar's vessel, and that our craft will be forfeit when the wager's lost. You're overlooking the fact that all we have to do is to win!"

Omar smacked his hand onto his forehead and uttered a vile oath. "One of you explain to this fool of a captain that there is no way we can beat a magical flying machine over that distance. Tell him in simple words, please, because I think our glorious leader's got sunstroke or something."

Rafi came up and laid a hand on Sinbad's forehead. "No. I'm afraid he's just the same as usual. Sinbad, you are aware of the nature of Anwar abd Anwar's amazing flying ship?"

"It's a silver carriage held aloft by a bag of gas," Sinbad answered. "The sorcerer summons zephyrs from his Bag of Winds to push it through the air."

"Foul sorcery," muttered Ralf Gunarson. He was not comfortable with the decadent sorceries of the civilized lands, so distant from the cold shamanic runes of his native North.

"It is a most puissant vessel that is said to be unmatched for speed," Tishimi Osara noted.

Sinbad gestured at the sleek Blue Nymph that bobbed at harbor in the teeming seaport. "We have a ship that gets pushed along by the wind as well," he argued. "There's no other like it in the world. Nothing is as fast, as graceful, as clever on the water. With a brave crew and a brilliant captain there's nowhere we can't go and nothing we can't accomplish."

"We can't fly," Henri Delacrois pointed out bluntly. "The Nymph's fast, I'll grant you, and despite your best efforts you haven't sunk her yet. But she can't sail over land. To reach the Sapphire Isle by sea we'll have to sail all round the coast. Anwar's Midnight Star can glide in a straight line all the way there."

"Well, that depends on how well he can navigate," Sinbad objected, "and how much magic he actually has to push that thing along at speed. I say we have a fighting chance, and that's why I made the bet with him. That and one other reason."

"What other reason?" demanded Omar in a tell-us-the-worst voice.

Sinbad told them.

They prepared to sail.

The Street of Thieves was not a good place for a man with a bag full of rubies and a sackful of gold dust to walk, but Sinbad was protected by one thing: he was going to see Ra's al Sâlouk, the king of scoundrels.

Ra's awaited him in the Beggar's Court. A hundred street-spies had alerted the master-rogue to Sinbad's coming. "So you have returned again, sailor," the scarred thief-lord declared.

"So it seems. Here's your money." Sinbad passed over the bag of rubies, payment with interest for the loan that had financed his most recent voyage.

Ra's admired the jewels, but his eyes were on Sinbad's gold. "You seem to have turned a profit, my old partner," he observed.

"I generally do. It's a knack. But on my return to Baghdad this time I find things unpleasantly changed."

Ra's al Sâlouk gestured round the Beggars Court. "The city endures. I still reign where any shadow falls."

"There are rumors that Caliph Haroun al-Rashid is sick, that he has taken to his bed and sees no-one save his closest advisors."

"I have heard those rumors."

"They also say that if he dies, half a dozen princelings and satraps wait poised to vie for the caliphate, and a score behind them waiting to tear at the scraps."

"That is so."

Sinbad drew in his breath. "With Haroun's illness his grip on Baghdad weakens. No-one now gives alms to the poor."

Ra's nodded sagely. "It is sad to see the destitute unable to keep up with their debts."

"You have taken many of them as slaves."

"They did not make their payments when the time was due. The law is clear on the matter."

Sinbad shook his head. "The city needs no more widows worked to death in the weaving sheds, nor children sold to the bordellos. You must not do this, Ra's al Ŝâlouk."

The prince of scoundrels smiled unpleasantly. "And who will stop me?" he challenged.

Sinbad didn't answer directly. Instead he opened the sack of Libyan gold dust and showed it to Ra's. "I will buy them from you," he declared. "All of them. For this."

Ra's raised a cynical brow. "You'll pay for the street-scum to be free? Why?"

"I've been a slave. I didn't like it. They'll be free, Ra's al Ŝâlouk – one way or another."

If the master-rogue heard the threat behind the sailor's words he pretended to ignore it. "Done!" he agreed. He turned to his bravos. "Set the prisoners free. Commend them to the care of bold Captain Sinbad."

The destitute captives came from the cellars in frightened huddles, blinking into the light after days or weeks of confinement. Some were little more than walking skeletons. "Go to my house, the green-tiled mansion on the Street of Fountains," Sinbad told them all. "There is a porter there with the same name as I, Sinbad. Tell him I have sent you. He'll see you fed and clothed and healed, and you will be given what you need for a new start."

Ra's watched the sailor with contempt. "No wonder you are always penniless," he scorned. "No wonder you had to make such a foolish wager with the Clockwork Sorcerer."

"I've won much and lost much in my time," Sinbad answered him, "but today at least I have done the right thing."

There was a holiday atmosphere at the docks. Word of Sinbad's wager with the Clockwork Sorcerer had spread like wildfire, and thousands turned out to see the race begin. Already money was changing hands about who would reach the Sapphire Isle first, but those who wanted to bet on Sinbad got much better odds.

Many of the notables of Baghdad had made the journey down to the seaport to watch the contest begin. Sage Geber, surely the greatest alchemist ever to live, Grand Master of the Thaumaturge's Guild, arrived in person to proclaim the start of the race.

Sinbad joined him on the platform, clad in his fanciest silks with an inlaid sapphire pinned to his turban. Anwar abd Anwar still outdid him though, arriving in a palanquin pulled by metal horses of cunning clockwork, escorted by footmen of bronze who whirred and clicked as they led their master to the stage.

Sinbad bowed deeply at the Clockwork Sorcerer, then proffered an oil can to the preening wizard. The crowd laughed.

"We must review the terms of the wager," Sage Geber insisted. He wasn't a great public speaker – his students suspected he chose to mumble and speak in obscurities so they had to think hard – but the alchemist's authority was absolute. The huge audience on the dockside fell silent. "The dispute is over the relative speeds of two vehicles owned respectively by Anwar abd Anwar and Sinbad the Sailor. Sinbad's ship is the Blue Nymph, a sea vessel of Ethiopian teakwood of most remarkable design. The Clockwork Sorcerer's sky-boat is of silver and crystal, with a silken canopy that bears it high aloft, a wonder and marvel to all who see it."

Sinbad squinted up at the great airship floating above the docks. "Could do with a wash," he commented loud enough to be heard.

"The vessels shall prove themselves in a race to the distant and mystical Sapphire Isle," Geber continued. "Although usually warded from mortal visitation, by diligent negotiation with the Lords of the Brass City this earthly fortress of the mighty djinn will be opened to our competitors. Whichever competitor reaches there first will win the gamble – and the vessel of the other."

Omar mouthed the word idiot at Sinbad from the deck of the Blue Nymph.

"I think additionally, the loser should have to shave off his unfortunate beard," Sinbad added.

Anwar abd Anwar looked at him sharply. "You hardly have a beard" he objected. The sailor had a moustache and neatly trimmed Van Dyke.

"And yet," grinned Sinbad. The crowd laughed with him again.

"Enough!" snapped the Clockwork Sorcerer. "This farce has gone on too long. Let this insolent adventurer learn the folly of his ways. How he will return from the Sapphire Isle, none can say. He shall receive no help from me. Let him become Sinbad the Swimmer!"

"Oh, don't be sore," Sinbad told the mage. He leaned in and clasped Anwar's wrist in a firm shake then hugged the surprised sorcerer and clapped him on the back. "Let the best man win, eh?"

Sinbad beat a hasty retreat before Anwar's clockwork retainers could get to him. Sage Geber raised his hands for silence. "I have lit a brazier atop the Tower of Thaumaturgy," the alchemist spoke. "It will burn day and night until Sinbad or Anwar reaches the Sapphire Isle. Thereafter it will flare and blaze, red if the Clockwork Sorcerer is victorious, green should Sinbad triumph. In this way all shall know which vessel has prevailed."

"And when we get back we'll bring merchandise from the djinn," Sinbad announced to the crowd. "We're running empty on the way out, of course, but get ready for some amazing produce when we get home again."

"You will not be back!" Anwar abd Anwar hissed. His straggly grey whiskers twitched in annoyance. "This time you will never return!"

"If there is nothing more of consequence to say," Geber interrupted pointedly, "then it is time to begin. When I touch off this flare you may launch your ships."

He counted down from five then ignited the flash powder.

Sinbad waved at the crowd then vaulted over the platform rail, caught a lanyard, and swung over the heads of the audience to drop neatly onto the foredeck of the Blue Nymph. "Cast off, Omar!" he called.

"Casting off!" the first mate confirmed. "Ralf, Henri, let slip the ropes. Tishimi, Haroun, trim the sail! Rafi, steer her three points to starboard. We're off!"

The sleek vessel came to life, twisting away from the dock with an easy grace, catching the wind like a racehorse scenting a chase. She rode the tide and darted away over the azure water.

The Clockwork Sorcerer's automatons bundled him back into his carriage and set the metal horses to drag him up to the mooring of his airship.

❦ ❦ ❦

"With fair winds we'll be at the Sapphire Isle in three days," Omar reported. "That's *with* fair winds and good navigation. Right now the breeze is quartering us from larboard and is failing."

"It was a great departure, Sinbad," Henri Delacrois admitted, "It made us look good in all the right ways. But now we can never go back there. The Nymph would be confiscated. We'll have to run back to Europe, to the waters near my Gaulish homeland."

Tishimi disagreed. "A wager has been made. It would be dishonorable not to pay the debt, however great it is."

Sinbad leaned on the prow of the Blue Nymph and addressed the figurehead that gave the ship her name. "Do you see how little faith my crew has in me, lady? They think I've made a dumb bet and I'm going to lose you like I usually lose whatever treasure I bring home from my voyages. As if I'd risk you if it wasn't life and death – and if I didn't have an edge!"

"An edge?" Ralf Gunarson echoed. The big Norseman didn't like losing. "What kind of an edge?"

Sinbad reached into his jacket and pulled out a velvet sack. "Anyone know what this is?" he asked his crew.

Rafi stared at the container and clapped his hands to his cheeks. "That looks an awful lot like Anwar abd Anwar's Bag of Winds," he observed. "The magical sack that summons the zephyrs that push along his air-boat."

"Yes," agreed Sinbad el Ari. "It fell out of his pocket when we were hugging and somehow dropped into my tunic."

"You stole it!" Tishimi accused.

"You stole it!" Henri approved. "Whatever it is."

Omar took the velvet sack from his captain. "This is how the Clockwork Sorcerer binds up winds to use for his navigation," the first mate said. "He's boasted of it. It's not his own creation, of course, but magic he's traded for the cunning devices he's wrought. Without this he'll find it much harder to get the Midnight Star to her destination ahead of us."

"So we could use this to speed our voyage?" Henri exclaimed. A happy smirk blossomed on his face. He'd thought the Byzantine ducats he'd placed on the Blue Nymph's victory to be lost coin.

"Hope so," admitted Sinbad.

Rafi sounded a note of caution. "Be careful, my friends. All winds are capricious, not to be trusted. Magic is more capricious still. If you use this Bag of Winds, let there be caution."

"Caution is my finest quality," Sinbad promised, wrenching open the mouth of the sack. "Caution and… knots?"

"Knots are your best quality?" Ralf puzzled. Sometimes the Moors' complex liquid language still confused him.

Sinbad showed him the bag. It contained three red cords each tied into a complicated hitch and pulled as tight as a noose. "Knots."

"I think I know this," Rafi pondered. "The ancient Greeks used this kind of magic, to bind things, just like Solomon the Great used his bottles and amulets. Spirits and sorcery were pent up in the ravel, and could not escape until the knot was unpicked."

"Alexander the Great cut the Great Knot at Gordium," Sinbad remembered.

"And the spirit he released entered him and conquered the known world," Rafi countered. "I say again, use caution."

"And fingernails," added Henri, who'd slipped one of the red cords out of the bag and was trying to loosen it. "This is impossible."

"I think we'll need to release one of these to get the wind we need," Sinbad admitted, "but let's be ready. Omar, batten the hatches. Secure everything like you would for a storm. Cleat the sail. I want everyone lashed to something secure so we're not tossed overboard. Then we'll undo a knot."

The crew of the Blue Nymph made hasty preparation. The natural winds had dropped to almost nothing and the ship barely moved over the coastal waters. Something had to be done or the race was forfeit.

When all was ready, Sinbad struggled with the tangled cord. For some time. "Um, Tishimi?" he asked at last, plaintively.

The warrior woman took the knot. Sinbad had expected her to use her shapely fingernails to pick it loose. Instead she tossed the cord in the air, drew her father's sword with a swift, fluid movement, and sliced right through the cleat, spilling the red string to the deck in eight pieces.

"It was good enough for Macedonian Alexander," Tishimi said defensively.

A wind stirred the chopped remnants, pushing them across the boards of the foredeck.

"This is not the time of year for trade winds," Omar admitted, "and yet…"

The Nymph's sail billowed out, catching the fresh breeze. The ship keeled. Henri shifted the wheel to keep her steady.

A hard wind set in, pushing the little vessel forward. "It's working!" Sinbad cried with delight.

Knots.

"Didn't you expect it to?" Ralf asked.

Sinbad shrugged.

"You are too lucky by half," Tishimi told the sailor; but as she turned the wind shifted, buffeting the Blue Nymph from a different quarter, pushing her over hard.

"Look forward!" Rafi cried out, terrified. "Lady Tishimi, turn to face the prow, quickly!"

The Japanese girl did as she was bid. The gale shifted again, returning to its former setting.

"Keep looking that way," Sinbad told her emphatically. Now they knew how the magic worked.

The winds pushed harder. The ship's mast creaked as it took the strain of the near-hurricane. The Nymph skipped lightly over turbulent seas, riding the great swells that now chased them, sliding through the foam like a dolphin. Henri called for Ralf to aid him with the wheel.

Sinbad climbed to the prow, where the spume could wash over him and the wind pushed him onward, and he laughed.

The tempest drove them on for a day and a night, until the crew struggled to set the ship aright in the constant winds and exhilaration was replaced with exhaustion. When the winds fell from gale to gust and from gust to desultory breeze Sinbad allowed all but a light watch to take some rest.

Four hours later he severed the second knot and pushed the Blue Nymph forward again, surging over a roiling sea towards the Sapphire Isle.

Henri was relieved at the wheel by Omar and came to join Sinbad at the prow, rubbing his aching arms. "I confess I know little of this Sapphire Isle," he told his captain. "Is it too much to hope for sapphires?"

"No one knows much about it," Sinbad admitted. "Some think it merely an allegory, like the Philosopher's Stone that turns base metals to gold, or the Shamir worm that can cut its way through anything. Except Sage Geber has found both those things, so maybe this is an allegory we can dock at?"

"That clears that up then," the Gaulish archer snorted. "They say genies live there. Those are spirits, yes? Fairies?"

"Intelligences not of this world, say," Sinbad judged. "My people have many stories about them. We believe that Allah made three sentient races, the angels, we mortals, and the djinn. All three have free will to be good, bad, or indifferent. Angels are made of light, humans of matter. Djinn are fire. They are invisible to us except when they wish otherwise, and have terrible power[1]."

"So we're sailing to an island of beings we can't see who can destroy us at a whim?"

"Probably. Except that Solomon the Great defeated most of them and bound them. The greatest he sealed in bottles and rings and jewels, slaved to serve him, to grant his wishes. The rest were restricted by laws of behavior that limit how they can interact with this mortal world."

"Sage Geber said something about people not usually visiting Sapphire Isle."

Sinbad nodded. "We must really have caught the djinn's attention to be allowed there. It's supposed to be a half-way place between our realm and theirs."

Henri sighed. "Of all the fun places we could have raced to, you had to go pick some mythical island full of beings that can stomp us to paste whenever they feel like it."

"Yes."

Henri considered this in stoic silence for a while as the Blue Nymph scudded over the choppy sea. At last he said, "So *does* it have sapphires?"

❀ ❀ ❀

The second knot of wind pushed Sinbad on all day, only blowing its last fitful gusts as the sun sank low over the western ocean. No land was in sight now, but the lodestone still worked, twisting in its bowl of oil to show north, and with that and a sextant Sinbad was able to calculate a general position and plot a course.

Before the sun had finally vanished into the sea, Haroun the lookout called out and pointed ahead to where twin pillars marked the way to the Sapphire Isle. Sinbad remembered Geber's instruction. "We have to pilot the Nymph between those stones," he told Omar. "They are the gateway to another sea."

His first mate looked out at the huge pillars that rose from the sunset-colored ocean. They were shaped like hunched men or giant chess pieces, each standing a hundred and fifty feet above the waterline. Their chiseled surfaces were weathered and mottled, long overgrown with weed and

---

1   Sinbad's information comes from Sūrat al-Jinn (Arabic: سورة الجنّ), the 72nd sura of the Qur'an.

barnacles. Beyond them other stones and jagged walls rose up from a shallow sea.

"It would be easier to navigate round," Omar suggested. "There looks to be lots of sunken debris there. Why risk tearing the bottom out of the Nymph when we can circle and pass on?"

"Sage Geber was specific in his instructions to Anwar and I. Even the Clockwork Sorcerer must pilot his air-boat right between those two statues. It is the only way to the Sapphire Isle."

Ralf glowered at the thick high markers as the ship sailed up to them. "How does this Geber know so much of these genies anyway?" the Norseman demanded suspiciously. "How do we know we can trust a wizard?"

Rafi came to the defense of the great alchemist. "If any wise man can be trusted, it is Abu Mūsā Jābir ibn Hayyān[2]. He helped the Abbasids to power in Persia, and is personal friend of his patron, the Great Caliph Haroun al-Rashid, may Allah ever smile upon him! Geber is the author of three thousand books on everything from astrology to music, biology to grammar. He wrote the Kitab al-Zuhra and the Kitab Al-Ahjar[3] and the Ten Books on Rectification which describe the alchemists Pythagoras, Socrates, Plato and Aristotle."

"Well I'd never heard of him till I came to Baghdad," Ralf retorted. "One wizard's much the same as another to me."

"You'd never heard of washing, either," Rafi shot back. "Geber invented the retort and the alembic and discovered crystallization and distillation. He identified citric acid, acetic acid, tartaric acid, antimony, arsenic, bismuth, brimstone, even mercury. He has taught the making of salts, of nitric and sulfuric acids, of aqua regia and saltpeter. No education in medicine or alchemy is complete without an understanding of Geber's teachings."

---

2   Abu Mūsā Jābir ibn Hayyān, known more commonly by his Persian name Geber, was the Abbasid era's most prominent scientist and scholar. All the things attributed to him in the conversation between Sinbad and Rafi here are generally held to be true, although many of his books may have been collected rather than authored by him. Geber was revered in medieval Europe as the founder of alchemy and is remembered now as the originator of many important chemical processes. If Caliph Haroun al-Rashid had anyone who could be called a Sage, it was the polymath Geber.

3   *The Book of Venus* and *The Book of Stones*, two of the most important works of medieval alchemy and early chemistry.

"Geber is famous," Sinbad admitted, "and usually pays top price for any strange substances I drag back from my voyages. I trust him, or we wouldn't be here."

Tishimi leaned over the rail and stared up at the huge statues. "Did he say what these things were?" she wondered.

The Blue Nymph sailed between the sentinels. "Gates to another ocean, he claimed," Sinbad answered. "From here our course lies due west for a night and a day, but we won't be able to use the last wind-knot because the seas are shallow with many rocks."

The dying light of the sun glinted off rusted metal archways that broke the sea's surface. "I think this was a city once," guessed Henri.

"Whatever it was I want someone at the prow with a fathoming chain," Omar called practically. "And sharp lookouts." Nobody suggested anchoring for the night.

Tishimi looked back at the giants they had passed. "I thought I saw movement up there," she confessed. "Do birds nest on those high ridges?"

"Or perhaps they're something else." Henri turned to look where the girl had pointed, then strung his bow.

He was just in time. The first of the attackers was already launching itself from the heights towards the Blue Nymph.

"Beware!" Henri called. He loosed a shot even as he gave warning, but the arrow clattered uselessly off the metal carapace of the monstrous thing that dropped towards the ship.

There were four devices, each roughly the size of a horse, winged and clawed in the semblance of gryphons, constructed from sheet copper and cunning cogs. They swooped down on the ship, tearing at her azure sail and rigging.

"Anwar abd Anwar has set a trap for us!" Sinbad called to his comrades. He sliced a rope to release the jib and pull him upwards to the first of the clockwork monsters. He vaulted onto its back, riding it like a bronco. "It makes sense he'd send assassins ahead to lurk here. It's the only place he could guarantee we'd pass!"

The flying monster bucked, but Sinbad was able to jam his dagger between the plating covering the gears at its neck. There was a hard grinding sound and the metal wings seized. As the machine plunged down into the sea, Sinbad leaped to the next gryphon.

Another of the creatures dropped to the deck, its iron jaws champing to tear prey. Ralf slammed into it from the side. His massive strength actually managed to topple the mechanism on its flank. Omar dived forward to pin the creature with a spear. Tishimi's katana pierced the monster's metal sheath and severed its inner workings.

Sinbad's second ride tried to toss him. "A rope!" the sailor called to Haroun in the crow's nest. The boy hurled a coil to his captain. Sinbad looped it round the automaton's neck then jumped again, managing to catch onto the final monster's swishing tail.

The creature swung round, easily able to reach the dangling attacker with its jaws and claws. A flight of shafts from Henri did it no harm but distracted the automaton long enough for Sinbad to knot a rope around the monster's legs before diving down into the sea.

Now the two remaining gryphons were yoked together, tangled in Haroun's rope. The more they struggled the more they worked against each other, fouling their wings and losing altitude. One of them made for the boat, intent on latching its claws onto the Nymph's side. Ralf shouldered it off into the ocean.

Sinbad swam to the ship and Rafi hauled him aboard. The clockwork monsters were too heavy to rise again from the waters.

"Repair the sail," Omar called to the other crew. "Let's be out of here before anything else can catch us."

The sun set. The Blue Nymph picked her way through the flooded ruins, setting course ninety degrees to port of the constant shining Pole Star.

The race was still on.

Sinbad woke from his bunk at noon. The ship had long since cleared the ruins. The Blue Nymph now sailed other seas than those of the mortal world. The ocean reflected the high sun with a metallic tint and the air smelled hotter and more raw. The ship handled differently, washed by waves of unusual rhythm that made even experienced sailors queasy like first time sea-travelers.

Sinbad checked his ship. Henri had the helm. Rafi and Tishimi were hunkered down on the main deck examining the clockwork creature that the warrior girl's sword had wrecked.

Sinbad asked how they were getting on. "It makes no sense," Tishimi complained. The daughter of the famous swordsmith Tokami Osara had a good understanding of all things forged. The automaton baffled her. "There is no way that these things should move. There are springs and gears and pistons, but nothing to power them. It shouldn't have been able to fly. It shouldn't have been able to see and hear and think."

"Magic," Sinbad answered with a shrug.

"Magic has its laws as do all things, captain," Rafi pronounced. "If we can discern what rules this device has to obey it may help us with another attack. But... I confess it's not looking likely."

"Speaking of more trouble from Anwar abd Anwar," Sinbad considered, "Henri, if the Midnight Star should show up try and get a threaded arrow into it. If we attach a cable we could swarm up there."

"Sounds insanely dangerous to me," the Gaul answered, "so I expect you'll do it."

The talking woke the big Norseman Ralf. He snorted once and sat up quickly, reaching for a war-axe before he remembered where he was. "Ah," he sighed. "It wasn't a drunken dream then."

"No," Sinbad told him. "We really are about a half day away from an outpost of the djinn. Although I admit this whole voyage is taking on a dreamlike quality, as if we're drifting away from the things that make everyday sense. Geber warned me it might feel like that."

"Most of what the Sage says doesn't make sense," Omar complained. "His very name's given us a new word: gibberish.[4]"

"Knowledge gained too easily is held too lightly," Rafi protested.

Tishimi laid down the mainspring she'd detached and gave up on the clockwork gryphon. "Whatever magic worked this thing has gone now. You may as well heave it overboard and lighten the ship."

Ralf was happy to see the back of the thing. He called a pair of burly Sindhi crewmen and began the task of levering the carcass over the side.

"What should we anticipate when we reach the Sapphire Isle, Captain Sinbad?" Tishimi wondered. "Will we be expected to bring gifts of tribute, as if we were meeting our ancestors or visiting an emperor?"

Sinbad shrugged. "Geber couldn't tell me – which isn't the same as him not knowing, of course. What he did say I don't want to repeat aloud for the same reason I don't want to mention the reason for the wager. Not now we're through the pillars on the Sea of Brass."

Tishimi nodded acknowledgement. "As long as you know, I am content to trust you."

Sinbad ignored Henri's muttered "How have you lived this long?"

"There are three things worth mentioning though," Sinbad added. "The djinn value truth and despise lies. They keep their word if they give it, but they'll hold the letter and trick you if they can. And like men, they are

---

4   Geber's coded manuscripts made no sense to those not versed in his teachings and indeed gave modern English the work for nonsense; ironically the material labeled as gibberish was actually valuable scientific data.

good and bad, kind and cruel, helpful and harmful – sometimes all in one person. When we treat with them we'll have to be very careful."

"Will Sinbad be doing the talking for us?" Ralf asked in dismay.

"Keep sailing west," said Sinbad gruffly.

"Land ho!" shouted Haroun, pointing five degrees to port. "I can see a glistening blue rock jutting out of the sea!"

"Glistening like a sapphire?" checked Henri Delacrois. "Like a great many sapphires?"

Sinbad jumped up on the mast for a better view. "Take us in, Omar. Everyone stand ready."

"Aft!" called Haroun again, jabbing his arm straight behind the Blue Nymph. "In the sky!"

All eyes turned to the orange and silver horizon, where a tiny speck was moving like a seabird, closing fast.

"Tell me that's not the Midnight Star," Omar growled. "I thought this had been too easy."

"Too easy?" objected Sinbad. "I had to fight three mechanical gryphons. In the air!"

Tishimi strained to see the closing airship. "It seems as though you may have the opportunity again," she noted.

As the sky-ship approached them it became clear how it moved so swiftly. A silken sack of rare gases held the Midnight Star aloft, but it was towed along by six brass gryphons with furious sweeps of their metal-feathered wings.

"All sail!" called Sinbad. "Jib the bowsprit. Double-leaf the mains'l! Get this lady moving!"

Henri glanced at the distant Sapphire Isle and at the fast-closing Midnight Star. "I don't think we can reach land in time."

Ralf calculated the direction of the airship. "I don't think that's going to be our big problem," he warned, selecting a two-handed axe in preparation for trouble.

The Star veered closer. Two of the clockwork gryphons dropped their towing harnesses and wheeled into attack dives. They spiraled down from opposite sides, flanking the Nymph.

"All hands brace for boarders!" Sinbad called.

The starboard gryphon came in fast, raking the deck with outspread wings, sweeping crew right off the ship. It powered straight for Omar at the wheel.

Rafi gave a shout and mariners hurled the fishing nets. The ropes fouled the monster's mechanical wings for a moment, turning the power-dive at Omar into a roll-spin that ended with a hard crash into the rear cabin door.

Unharmed, the downed automaton sprang up ready for battle.

Ralf went in first, his axe scoring the engraved plates across the creature's shoulders. As the gryphon snapped at him, Tishimi came in on its blind-side, hoping to repeat her devastating blade puncture. This time the automaton was ready, though; its barbed tail swung round and hammered her hard. She was pounded off into the sea.

For a moment the Norseman stood alone. The huge flying lion-scorpion-eagle loomed above him, its gears racketing in a mechanical growl. Ralf did not back away. If this was his death he would enter the feasting hall of his gods unashamed.

Sinbad tumbled past, jabbing a dagger into one vulnerable leonine leg joint. When the automaton reacted, Henri was able to finesse a pair of steel-tipped Byzantine arrows into other chinks in the mechanism.

A cry from Haroun atop the mast warned that the other gryphon had arrived. This one landed on the sail crossbeam, padding with a cat's balance towards the crow's nest. But worse, tethered to it was a long thin thread that connected back to the Midnight Star. Already more machines were sliding and falling down that umbilical, using the rope to guide them unerringly to the Blue Nymph.

"Clockwork soldiers!" Haroun warned. "Like the things Anwar had attending him at the starting ceremony!"

More deadly mechanical killers! Already the first pair had rattled to the deck, rising unfazed from their near free-fall. They carried scimitars in each hand and stood ready to fight.

"Ignore them," Sinbad called to Henri. "Get the thread!"

The Gaulish archer understood at once. As dangerous as the automatons already on board might be, the dozen reinforcements that now descended the cord were worse! He turned his back on the approaching mechanical men and the rampaging monster on deck and loosed a shaft at the thin line between the gryphon on the square sail and the distant skyboat above.

The first flight nicked the rope but did not sever it. Another mechanoid slid to ground and joined the others in fighting the Nymph's beleaguered crew. Henri shot again. The second arrow sliced the thread clean. The rope fluttered away from the gryphon that anchored it. The fast-descending machine monsters tumbled helplessly into the sea.

Sinbad hadn't finished with the archer yet. "The ties securing the sail!" he called to Henri. "Sever them!"

The Gaul saw what was required. Haroun was trapped, trying to fend off a ferocious automaton aloft with nothing more than a seaman's knife. The lad had no chance. It was a wonder that the segmented scorpion's tail hadn't already shredded the agile young lookout.

On the ground, Rafi and Omar fought losing battles against implacable non-living guardsmen. Sinbad grappled the gryphon on the main deck, scrabbling between its thrashing wings, trying to avoid the sweeping jabs of its poisoned tail. Only Ralf had any luck; he scooped up the latest automaton guard, hoisted it above his head, then hurled the machine headlong over the side.

Henri concentrated on the cleats that held the mast's crosspiece in place. Long experience of the eccentric ship meant he knew exactly where to place his shots to cut through pulley ropes. A half dozen shafts sliced through one end, half-dropping the sail, toppling the gryphon away from Haroun. It fell to the deck but landed on its feet, wings spread out for balance.

Sinbad managed to maneuver the automaton he was riding to slam into the other. It caused a moment's chaos, helpful but too brief. Ralf swung his axe at the mechanical guard that cornered Rafi. The Norsemen half-severed its head. The machine made an unpleasant grinding noise then collapsed, a broken marionette.

Omar's adversary knocked the first mate's cutlass aside and closed in for the kill. Tishimi appeared unexpectedly to hurl herself in the way, parrying with her ancestor-sword. The warrior maid was soaked and bruised but had hauled herself back aboard for more.

Henri had no time to shoot again. The gryphon he had downed reared high then sprang right at him.

The crossbeam dropped on it from above, crashing into the machine with devastating weight. Haroun had released its other fastening. The African boxwood hammered deep dents into the automaton's bronze casing. The gryphon twitched and fell over, suddenly unable to use the pistons and gears down its left side. Ralf went in with axe and hammer.

Sinbad pulled off his turban and wrapped it as a rein and a blinder round the head of the creature he was riding. The thing thrashed even harder, jabbing with barbed poisoned tail, trying to destroy its unseen tormentor. He managed to get it to barrel into the remaining metal guard,

...the crossbeam dropped on it...

crumpling the clockwork soldier and knocking it aside useless. He called for another dagger and Omar hurled him one.

The gryphon did not like the katar's[5] prick in its cogs. It shuddered again, almost dislodging Sinbad, then slammed its scorpion tail round to skewer him once and for all.

Sinbad dodged. The automaton's barbed sting punched through its own back amour, lodging in its own vital mechanisms. The sailor rolled free at last as the machine destroyed itself. "I've seen scorpions do that to themselves sometimes," the breathless sailor confided – well, almost breathless; Sinbad could always find enough wind to speak.

Ralf waited for the right moment when the last struggling gryphon was off-balance to catch it and tip it through the Blue Nymph's guardrail and down into the Brass Sea.

"Did we just survive that?" asked Henri skeptically.

Haroun's urgent cry warned of the next threat. Fist-sized winged spheres buzzed down from the Midnight Star, whirring with malicious promise of death.

Whatever they were, Sinbad didn't want them on his ship. "Henri!" he called again.

The archer reached for the last shaft in his quiver. His shot caught the first of the golden spheres. The machine exploded in an ugly plume of Greek fire. The blast detonated the half-dozen globes that dropped with it, but there were others further out still closing on the Blue Nymph.

Aloft, Haroun called for buckets to douse the minor fires that smoldered in the torn rigging.

"Anwar wanted to capture the ship intact," Rafi guessed, "but now he just wants to win."

"He just wants us dead," Omar snarled, "May Allah cause his scraggly beard to grow ever inward!"

"I need more arrows," Henri called urgently as the next wave of golden spheres approached. "I don't know that I can stop them all!"

Sinbad looked around his damaged ship. With the mainmast unstrung there was no way of outrunning the winged globes. His crew were battered and exhausted from the automaton attacks. He had only once choice.

"All hands secure for a storm!" he called. "Everybody grab something! Get everybody out of the water!" He reached to his belt where the velvet Bag of Winds was lashed and pulled out the last knot.

5   A katar is a Persian hunting knife, also called a tiger knife for its use in killing big game. It has an unusual h-shaped hilt allowing it to be used in a punching motion to penetrate amour.

Rafi saw what the sailor intended. "Sinbad…!"

"No other choice, my friend," Sinbad said as he sliced apart the red knot.

Perhaps it was the urgent circumstances, or because the Blue Nymph now sailed in other waters, but this time the tempest broke around the ship immediately, without warning. Twenty-foot waves battered the hull. It was shaken like a fish in the mouth of a big cat. Omar struggled uselessly with the tiller wheel. The storm was absolute.

Sinbad saw Henri shout something that was doubtless cynical and Gallic, and thought Ralf mouthed some oath to the boreal gods of his frozen north, but voices could not carry over the howling storm.

Remembering that the hurricane before had pressed wherever its invoker faced, the sailor looked upward at the incoming spheres. The little delicate-winged golden balls were swept away. Some exploded as they tumbled.

Higher aloft the Midnight Star was suddenly beset with fierce winds beyond the capacity of the magic that sustained it. The airship shuddered and span helplessly, whirled like a leaf in a winter's gale. In the command gondola the Clockwork Sorcerer bent all his power to retain command of the hurricane-battered flying machine.

Sinbad waited until Anwar abd Anwar had wrestled control of his vessel then he suddenly looked downwards. The changed direction of the tormented air pressed the Blue Nymph low in the water, sinking her almost to her gunwales. When Sinbad turned his face upwards again he was gratified to see the Star had been knocked from her high altitude and now wavered unsteadily and lopsidedly mere yards above the foaming sea.

Tishimi tugged at his sleeve and mouthed something that looked like, "We're sinking." Sinbad nodded and turned direction again, hoping that the tempest would push his leaking ship ahead of the storm and beach it on the Sapphire Isle – before the Nymph shipped enough water to drag it beneath the ocean forever.

Hurriedly he ordered the crossbeam raised, hefting their blue canvas sail so that it once again caught air.

The Blue Nymph was driven forward, breaking through high waves that sent sheeted spray over the whole vessel. Sinbad couldn't turn to see what was happening with the Midnight Star. His whole focus now was on blowing his damaged ship to some part of shore where there were few rocks to tear her bottom out.

He was surprised when the winds vanished as quickly as they had come. The previous knot-gales had blown for the better part of a day. Here it was as if a great hand had covered the Blue Nymph, shielding her from the storm.

He looked around, puzzled.

Rafi appeared bedraggled and dripping, after his experience being caught under the collapsed sail. "We are come to the island," the barber-surgeon explained. "The djinn allow no crude tempest to prevail here. No mere wind spirit would dare to trespass upon their demesne."

Henri looked behind them, to where the sea still churned with a furious malevolence. "Look!" he called.

All the crew turned in time to see the Midnight Star slapped down into the ocean. She floated at first, but then the seventh wave hit her and she vanished beneath the boiling surface. She was not seen again.

"There goes my winnings," mourned Sinbad al Ari.

Ralf clapped him on the back, staggering him. "But that means you have won!"

Omar struggled to control the damaged Nymph. Automaton and tempest had left their marks on the battered barque. She was low in the water and listing to starboard. "We need to beach while we can," Sinbad's first mate warned. "Haroun?"

The sharp-eyed lad still somehow clung to the mast. "That way!" he pointed. "I think I see a shore."

"Get us there," Sinbad called. He climbed atop the mermaid figurehead and strained to see the narrow cleft that Haroun had spotted in the high forbidding cliffs of the landmass before them.

Omar had to exert all his skill to navigate the ship through the break in the rocks. What crew was not bailing were set to the oars to win the Blue Nymph more way and better maneuverability. With painful slowness the sinking barque passed through the cleft into a shallow lagoon with tropical sands.

The Blue Nymph lodged on a soft bank and settled with the air of a ship that was not going any further until she had received serious care and attention.

"We're here!" Sinbad proclaimed. "The Sapphire Isle!"

The Caliph of Baghdad's daughter looked at the traveler on her bed with wide-eyed amazement. "So you got there! You won your bet!"

"Of course, fairest of jasmine-blossoms," Sinbad told her, grinning. "How could you doubt me?"

"I doubt your whole tale, you rogue," the princess scorned, "but it was a grand story."

"Worth the price?" Sinbad asked her. "I believe there was mention of kisses?"

Beneath her gauzy veil, Ayisha's perfect tongue flicked over her perfect lips. "There may have been," the princess admitted.

She unhooked the side of her yashmak, revealing the beauty of her naked face. Her mouth glistened as she fastened it on Sinbad's.

The kiss was over too soon. Ayisha leaned away, watching to see what the sailor would do next.

"I was promised reward in proportion to how much my story pleased the most lovely of all women," Sinbad reminded her. "How pleasing did you find my tale?"

"It was an interesting conceit," the princess judged. "A complete fantasy, of course."

"But worth more than one kiss, I'd say."

"The kisses of a princess are rare and precious things. Your account amused, but there are many tale-spinners in my father's court."

"Oh, I'd hoped for a better review than that," the sailor told her. "Fortunately, my story's not yet done. Let's see if we can't make you warm to my tale more when I tell you what happened when we arrived on the Sapphire Isle."

He spread himself out alongside Ayisha and stroked his fingers over her smooth soft belly. "You see, we had scarcely arrived and beached ourselves…"

"We're here!" Sinbad proclaimed, "The Sapphire Isle!"

Even as he spoke the gentle lagoon around them changed. The air thickened, as it sometimes did before lightning. Complicated ripples pattered the haven basin. Even the light altered, reddening, casting uncomfortable shadows.

"What's this?" demanded Ralf. He fingered his axe. "Sinbad…?"

Tall ivory towers broke through the sand and rose high into the orange skies. Brass gates and horn palaces grew like weeds. Verdant terraces built themselves, with plants of subtle and haunting fragrance. Wild monkeys with faces too much like humans chattered from the palms.

What had seemed like mere rock became wrought masonry. Clumps of foliage turned into great basking cats in jeweled collars, their tails swishing angrily as they glared at the intruders. Last of all, gold-armored guards, half as tall again as mortal warriors, shimmered into sight at the portals and passing places of the djinn outpost.

"We're very definitely here," Henri agreed under his breath.

Rainbow ripples moved over the surface of the buildings. A rich spicy redolence filled the air. Somewhere in the distance were sonorous bells.

Rafi dropped to his knees. "Is this real or a dream?"

"Both, I think," judged Sinbad. "Geber said that no human eye could look on a djinni as it truly is, so we clothe them in things we can understand." He climbed up on the prow of the Blue Nymph and called to the city. "Great lords, I come with greetings from the Caliphate of Persia, with compliments from the Sage Geber and all the people. I thank you for your hospitality."

The air was filled with roaring as if a thousand voices spoke at once. Eventually they coalesced into one: "You have not yet been granted our hospitality."

Sinbad swallowed hard. "I've brought you gifts. Sage Geber offers his latest book, a treatise on the natural things of our world which may be novel and strange to you. And I have brought fine glassware from the East and rare painted eggs from the Steppes of Rus, and a scimitar that once belonged to the famous Al-ad-din."

The roar rose again. "You have not yet been granted our hospitality, Sinbad the Sailor, because you have not yet taken the Test."

"Test? Sage Geber didn't actually mention any test."

"Mortals do not come often or easily to the court of the djinn-lords," the voices chorused. "Nor has our experience of them been good."

"I would hope that great minds such as yours would judge each man on his own merit, not mistake one villain's infamy for the character of all."

The voices broke into a babble of confusion, until one deeper, louder speaker overwhelmed the rest. "Enough. Let the Rawun[6] decide. All secrets are known to her and no man may evade her sight."

---

6   This word literally means "reporters" or "narrators". Readers are at liberty to speculate why the djinn do not describe their seeress with the singular feminine conjugation *rawiyah*.

Sinbad bowed. "We would be most pleased to welcome your wise woman," the sailor promised. "We shall set out a gangway so that she may…"

"I am here," said a voice in his ear.

The Rawun was tall and stately, robed in embroidered robes of russet and saffron edged with gold thread. Her fringed veil covered all but eyes that might have been a child's or could have seen the birth of worlds. She did not appear on the foredeck amongst the travelers so much as seem to have always been there.

Sinbad bowed low and kissed her tattooed hand. "Great lady, you honor us with your…"

"I am not here to speak with you," the djinni seer cut him short. "You have concealed yourself so long and so well, living by your wits and deceptions, that you can no longer strip away your masks. I will ask another what I wish to know."

The Rawun's presence was irresistible. Omar, Ralf, Henri, Tishimi, Rafi, Haroun, every mortal present on the boat was captivated by her. Each one knelt waiting to see if she would pick him to testify, yearning and dreading her attention.

The Rawun ignored them all. She glided past Sinbad to the carved figurehead that gave his ship its name. "Speak," she bade it.

The Blue Nymph awoke and moved, curled round to look at the crew that she carried. Her lustrous hair shifted and coiled, covering and uncovering perfect round breasts. Her sea-colored eyes fixed on Sinbad.

"He is a rogue," she told the Rawun. "A trickster, a vagabond, a thief, a troublemaker. He is survivor of many mishaps and instigator of many plots." But then the Blue Nymph grinned. "He is also noble, bold, kind, firm in friendship, terrible in enmity. His is a hero to those whom none else will champion. His curiosity knows no bounds. His spirit can never be crushed."

"You approve of him, then," the Rawun asked the Nymph.

"Of course not," the figurehead declared with a giggle and a toss of her head, "but he is a good man and my true master, and I will bear him for as long as I may, as far as he wills."

"Why?"

The Nymph blushed. "Because I love him."

Sinbad looked up with tears in his eyes; but the Blue Nymph was just a wooden image of a fair mermaid attached to his vessel's prow.

The Rawun regarded him carefully. "No one may lie to me," she said.

"Let him be Tested, Grand Sultan."

The voices spoke again. "What Test, Rawun? Shall he face the pit of fire and battle against the raging efriit? Or endure the trial of many cuts, spilling his life's blood to show his bravery? Perhaps we shall cast his flesh into the underworld to face the ghuls that they may taste his heart? Or set him far in the desert at the Phoenix's pyre that her holy flames may burn away his deceptions?"

Sinbad raised his hand. "Excuse me, mighty ones. All of those tests sound terrible and painful, and I'm sure I'd take them to prove my worth if I had to. But I reckon the thing you want most from mortals isn't integrity or valor or wisdom or purity. I think you want entertainment. Isn't there some test you have that's less fatal and more interesting to watch?"

The susurrus of voices rose again, then fell silent.

"It is agreed," declared the Rawun. "You shall pass through the Catacomb of Mirrors."

The heat awoke Sinbad. His lips were cracked and dry, his mouth swollen with thirst. He stared up at a remorseless blue sky above a featureless endless ocean.

His body protested as he sat up. He was aboard the Blue Nymph, and skilled hands had repaired her from her recent damage. His crew lay sprawled around her deck, each as exhausted and parched as himself.

Sinbad crawled across to Omar and shook his faithful first mate. "Wake up. Where are we?"

The grizzle-bearded Sindhi blinked gummed eyes open and looked about. "I do not know," he confessed. His voice was raw and cracked.

"We were on the Sapphire Isle," Sinbad remembered. "At least I think we were. There was a chase, the Nymph versus the Midnight Star, and I loosed a storm. And then there were... djinn?"

His voice stirred Henri. "That must have been days ago," the archer croaked. He reached for his aching throat and winced at the sunburn he'd taken lying unprotected on the ship's deck. "What happened after that?"

"A Test," rasped Tishimi, struggling to hands and knees. "That's what the Rawun said. A test of worthiness. A Catacomb of Mirrors."

Henri groaned. He struggled over to the Nymph's waterskins and found them empty. "I think we failed."

Omar crawled over to the binnacle and peered into the oil bowl that housed the ship's lodestone compass. "We're drifting," he reported. "Just circling round on ourselves on this windless sea."

Sinbad leaned over the side and peered into the still waters. He did not recognize this ocean. The cloudless sky above reflected back to him, along with his own pinched face.

"No water aboard," Henri reported. "No provisions at all. We will not last long in this heat."

Rafi rolled over. It was all he could manage. "I think the djinn have set us here to die, far from home."

The sailors considered his words. Sinbad remembered all the other times he'd lost ships and comrades to misadventure. He'd started to dare hope that the Blue Nymph and her crew were different.

He made a decision. "I don't think we failed," he told his companions. "I think we're being tested now." He bellied forward over the side of the Nymph into the hot salt waters – the reflective salt waters, smooth and clear as a mirror.

"Wait!" Tishimi called, but Sinbad splashed into the endless ocean, below its surface, into a deep dark coolness, a liquid bliss.

He surfaced again in fresh water in a dim cavern. Green crystal lamps illuminated the stalagmites that rose from the reflecting pool. Cut steps led to a hinged door of polished malachite.

"It was the Test!" Sinbad told himself, for none of his people were present. He slumped back into the clean clear water and drank his fill.

When it became obvious that none of his crew were joining him he hauled himself onto dry land and padded to the carved door. It opened to his touch and led into a dark space beyond.

Sinbad detached one of the green lamps and lofted it before him. Only two paces into the space beyond the portal his hand slammed into something unseen. He felt forward and found the smooth surface of a glass wall, so finely wrought that even when he held the lamp beside it he could hardly discern the glazing was there.

Another such barrier barred his right, but the way left was open. Sinbad moved that way but two paces on struck another unseen wall. This time the side to the right was clear, so he traveled that way. Next he had to turn left, and thereafter found the ways on either side available to him although his passage straight forward was blocked.

"A maze of glass," the sailor realized. "The Catacomb of Mirrors."

Sinbad considered trying to leave a trail to help him trace his steps but he had little on him that would accomplish the task. He decided to rely upon his wits and memory and hope that his sense prevailed over the djinn's trap. But his next step took him to where the smooth glass floor was absent, tumbling him down to a hard landing on another transparent surface ten feet below.

The lantern shattered as it landed. Now Sinbad was in darkness except for distant candle-lights reflected from far above.

He remembered that he'd challenged the djinn to test him in a way that amused them.

For an undetermined time Sinbad pressed on, weaving randomly left and right through the maze. He thought that sometimes the path angled upwards as he trudged, but twice he narrowly avoided floor-gaps that would have tumbled him down to unknown depths.

He had no way of judging hours in the glass-filled darkness but it seemed like many passed before he came across an actual mirror. He flinched at first, believing that some assassin also lurked in the stygian labyrinth. Sinbad only realized he faced a reflection when his opponent reached for a jambiya[7] exactly as he did

"Hah. Nice to have some good company," he told the Sinbad in the glass.

Something more reflected behind that Sinbad. The sailor whirled round but could see nothing in the gloom. He turned back, and there was the image, brighter and clearer now.

"Ralf?" Sinbad recognized the tall fair-haired Norseman, leather vested, a greatsword on his hip, axe and war-hammer at his back. He looked just as the sailor had first encountered him at that nameless tavern in some obscure Mediterranean port, where Ralf had quarreled with his Viking ship-mates about returning without battle to their Northern home. This image of Ralf even had the great horn cup he'd held that day as he'd challenged the whole of Sinbad's crew to a drinking contest – and prevailed. Thereafter it had seemed churlish not to take the big stranded Viking onto the Blue Nymph, and Sinbad had never regretted it.

But why was he seeing Ralf now, reflected in the djinni's maze?

Sinbad's gaze flicked elsewhere for a moment. When he looked again the glass showed him a different scene. Ralf lay dead, his gull-picked body dumped on some shoreside refuse pile. His clothes and weapons were gone and his throat was slashed open where he'd been murdered from behind as he slept.

Sinbad didn't recognize the coastal town. There were so many crumbling shoreside villages dotting so many coasts, ruined echoes of the great ports they had been when the Romans ruled hundreds of years since,

---

7   A curved double-edged knife.

sinking back into poverty and desolation. Perhaps it was the same place that Sinbad had first encountered Ralf? If not it was somewhere like it, and the fierce Norseman had died there.

"Is this what would have happened if you'd not come with me?" the sailor wondered. "Murdered in your sleep while you snored drunk, robbed for your clothes and weapons? No glory, no deeds, no heroic end to show your quality? The straw death that condemns your people to exile in a cold cheerless hell far from the revels of your hero-fathers?" If so, Sinbad was glad he'd overcome his prejudice and found a place for the big fierce warrior aboard the Blue Nymph.

The glass had shown him enough. Sinbad pushed on, stumbling through the invisible maze. When another mirror loomed ahead he examined it with trepidation. Henri Delacrois was in this reflection, sleek and charming in his close-laced hunting leathers. The runaway forester had escaped as far as the Brittany coast when his lord's men had caught up to administer punishment on the handsome rogue. Henri's liege had little forgiveness for a scoundrel he'd discovered in his wife's bed. Sinbad had liked the cunning archer since he'd first seen Henri duck a soldier's spear and overturn a fisherman's stall on his pursuers.

As with Ralf, the reflection changed. Henri did not look so dashing dangling from a rope with a crow picking at him and maggots where his eyes had been. The wind rattled the metal cage that contained his bones at the lonely crossroads. "Is this what would have happened if we hadn't come to your aid that day in Brittany?" Sinbad wondered out loud. "Or is this the future yet to come?" It was impossible to say.

Henri's image faded back to darkness. Sinbad pressed on. He wondered if he must see all his friends die.

Omar al-Keenjhar was next. Sinbad's first mate looked younger in the mirror's reflection, the way he was when Sinbad had first met him. It was ten years since a callow spoiled wastrel-youth had set out to restore the fortune he'd frittered away, boarding a ship piloted by the solid Sindhi boatman. That adventure had miscarried when Sinbad had discovered the land he'd set a campfire upon was actually a whale's back, but after many trials honest Omar had eventually rescued the young man. Another mariner might have extorted much of a callow youth for passage home. Omar had instead cared for Sinbad and taught him enough of sailing to ignite a lifetime's passion for the sea and to give him his sobriquet.

That made the subsequent death-vision of Omar more disturbing still. The greybeard floated in tangled weeds on some sea bed, his drowned corpse bloated and crab-torn. He hands seemed to reach out for the surface far above him and the air he was denied. It was a mariner's death, but a watery end was never easy.

Sinbad tried to work out what he was seeing. Was this some consequence of fate twisting differently in one of his past exploits with Omar? Perhaps a different result of his second voyage's journey to the roc-guarded Valley of Diamonds, where Omar had rescued him from the giant bird's nest? Or some mischance during that third travel, when Sinbad had finally blinded and killed the black giant who had eaten most of his shipmates, then had lost almost all the rest but Omar to the monster's ferocious mate? There had been plenty of opportunities for Omar to find a watery grave during Sinbad's adventures. Or was this his fate yet-to-come?

Sinbad thought about all the times he'd survived shipwreck and danger and how few of his companions had. Omar's luck must be stretched thinner than a whisker.

His vision of young Haroun was swift and puzzling. The street-lad had never really explained his origins, signing up last voyage with Sinbad as so many hopeful youths did, in hopes of glory and fortune. Unlike too many of them, Haroun had survived the experience so far. Even rarer, he had volunteered to sail again, eager for more. Sinbad did not like the reflection of the enthusiastic young man lying in a pool of his own blood, a jeweled dagger in his back. The mirror gave no other clue to Haroun's fate.

Rafi was next, reflected in the embroidered robes of a marketplace barber-surgeon in crowded Byzantium, where he'd plied his trade, exchanging gossip with those he tended as if it were currency. Part healer, part dentist, part hair-cutter, part spy, Rafi had put his Greek education and native wit to good use in that most volatile of political environments – until he had learned too much. Sinbad well remembered that desperate chase through the narrow alleys of the old Roman capital, with black-robed kahin fanatics close behind and crusader warriors hunting them through the souks.

Rafi's reflected end was by fire, struggling against his chains as the pyre at his stake caught in his clothes, his hair. It was impossible to tell what oaths or prayers he screamed as his flesh was consumed.

Sinbad turned away, sickened. For a moment he thought he could smell the burning flesh. He stumbled off blindly to escape the sight of his wise companion becoming a giant candle – and fell straight through another gap in the smooth glass floor.

The drop seemed further this time. Sinbad landed awkwardly, twisted his leg, and slammed his head into a glass panel. Bright sparks filled his vision and he lost all sense of balance. When he recovered his vision he found himself looking at his own bloody face in another mirror, and behind him the black-mantled form of Tishimi Osara. She held her swordmaker father's last blade in her hand, bloody as it had been that night when she'd slain the alley assassins who'd waylaid Sinbad; his first introduction to the sword-maiden's mysteries.

Sinbad's sight blurred again. When he refocused, it was Tishimi's death he saw. The graceful Japanese maiden lay on a bloody bed in a torn shift, her knife plunged into her breast, her own hands clutched around the hilt. Sinbad knew something of the circumstances of Tishimi's flight from her homeland; her father had died to withhold her from a feudal warlord who claimed her as concubine. Was this the end Tishimi would have given herself if she had not escaped Batu Kamito's grasp, or another threat of doom to come? Sinbad had heard the ancestor-vow the warrior maiden had taken to return and avenge her father's death on the man who had slaughtered him. Was this to be the cruel outcome?

The sight of Tishimi's lifeless face clawed at the sailor's courage. Sinbad wriggled away from the mirror, not wanting to see more, not yet able to trust his leg to hold his weight. Whatever amusement the djinn might be getting from these macabre looking glasses, Sinbad was not enjoying his Test.

The worst was to come, though. In the next mirror Sinbad saw himself.

It wasn't a plain reflection. This was the young man he had been, that arrogant wastrel who had frittered a prince's inheritance on amusements and fripperies, who had pursued pleasure with no thought for others and had cared for nothing but his own delight. If Sinbad the Sailor could have reached through the glass he would have throttled that self-centered youth with his bare hands.

"He knew nothing," Sinbad spat as he watched the crestfallen youngster turned away by those he'd thought his friends. His fortune gone, those who had helped him spend it had no more time for him. The mirror flashed a brief image of desperate young Sinbad signing aboard a trade boat for Africa, his last possessions bartered for a last desperate chance to recover his wealth.

That had been the journey with the whale, and the murderous water-breathing horse that preyed on the King of Etheop's breeding mares. Sinbad had lived a year in that fierce wild country before his ship had come to port and Omar had redeemed him.

Tishimi's lifeless face clawed at his courage.

Images of his second voyage were no more comforting. Sinbad glimpsed himself again being carried by the massive roc to feed her nest of fledglings, and saw anew the wonders and horrors of the Valley of Diamonds.

That terrible black giant with the boar's tusks and hot-coal eyes dominated his third journey. Sinbad was forced to watch again as his companions were eaten one by one.

He turned aside from the tormenting mirror only to find another glass behind him. His fourth voyage ended in shipwreck amongst cannibals who enslaved the castaways with mind-numbing herbs and fattened them for the pot.

"No..." Sinbad moaned. He knew what would come next but his eyes were transfixed. He watched himself abandon his enslaved fellows and scramble half-mad to the shore where he alone was rescued by gatherers from the nearby Island of Peppers.

As Sinbad stumbled on through the Catacomb of Mirrors, whichever glass he bumped into continued his tale.

Learning little from his previous follies, the young explorer had squandered his wealth once more – although offering more to charity now he had tasted poverty – and took to sea again to revisit the Valley of Diamonds. His companions' greed in breaking and devouring a roc's egg led to the destruction of their ship and each man's death, and to Sinbad's enslavement by the Old Man of the Sea. The glass images reminded Sinbad of the impossible goblin that latched itself to his back and rode him day and night for weeks of torment.

"I deserved it," Sinbad confessed. "It was my greed that led those others to their deaths, my failure to learn my lessons that led me to slavery."

His desperate raft journey down an unknown river took him to the rich land of King Serendib[8], where Sinbad's tales of Haroun al-Rashid's court so impressed that the traveler was sent home as a rich envoy bearing gifts for the ruler of Persia. Wealth, fame, success and royal favor fell to the wanderer; his companions all received unmarked graves on a forgotten shore.

Sinbad looked at his hands and realized they were bleeding where he had shattered the glass that showed him the sights.

"I *have* learned," Sinbad told the mirrors. "It took so long, so much blood, but I learned. I provided for the widows and orphans of my crews. I made right what I could and raised prayers to Allah for what I could not. I have tried to do good hereafter!"

---

8   Ceylon

There was more to see, of Sinbad and the blue ocean nymph, of Sinbad and the iron fleet, of the moment when Sinbad and Omar had determined to build the best ship that had ever sailed the oceans, of their subsequent adventures as they gathered together the crew that now followed Sinbad on his wild quests.

Sinbad closed his eyes to it. He suspected now that the mirrors were another trap, tearing at his conscience, stabbing his soul. He moved forward by touch alone, running his bloody hands along the glass surfaces, seeking out gaps, pressing forward. He did not know what nightmare glimpses of his past or future the mirrors showed him. He only moved on.

"If the point of all these reflections where to show me what I was, I already know," Sinbad called to the djinn. "I carry my failures and regrets with me wherever I travel. But I'm a sailor. I don't pack anything I do not need. I use what I have learned, learned at the cost of my blood and other men's, and I strive now for what's right. Do I best honor fallen comrades by lying down to die beside them or by struggling on and completing the work they began? Should the fact I have done ill in the past prevent me from doing good now?"

His searching hands groped ahead but found nothing save empty air.

He knew he must open his eyes.

Sinbad had reached the end of the labyrinth. A carved underground chamber contained six more mirrors, each reflecting again the death of one of his present companions. The Rawun awaited him there, her young-ancient face veiled and shadowed.

"You have almost found your way to the Court of the Djinn, Sinbad the Sailor," she proclaimed. "Your way there lies through any one of these mirrors. But shatter it and step through and you shall have your audience."

Sinbad regarded the silver glasses suspiciously. "What happens if I smash one?" he checked. "To the person in the mirror, I mean?"

"That person will meet that fate," the Rawun revealed. "You have sacrificed companions before on your voyages, Sinbad. What is one more?"

"I've never chosen to kill them," Sinbad protested. "I've been profligate and foolhardy, yes, but never a murderer of my comrades."

"You have an important reason to enter the Djinni Court."

"You know all truth. You know I do."

"Far more important than a boastful wager. That was designed only to catch our attention, to persuade us to allow you to come here so you could make your plea."

"Yes. Geber said you'd never let me get to the Sapphire Isle unless I entertained you."

"Entertain us, then," the Rawun told Sinbad. "Choose a mirror and step through."

"I can't!" the sailor protested. "Look, if you know why I'm here, you know how important it is. Haroun al-Rashid, may Allah preserve him as Caliph of Baghdad, ruler of Persia, is dying. Geber believes it to be a Ghul curse, a black sorcery by one of the fallen outcast undead of your race. I must plead with your Great Sultan for a cure, for a means of breaking the spell that saps our ruler's health and life."

"If it is so important then you will make the necessary sacrifice."

"Look, I know mortal affairs must seem very small and distant to you. I know your kind were hurt and constrained by the Binding of Solomon. But if you could only see Baghdad under Caliph al-Rashid, what it is become – a place of art and music, of poetry and science, a city of delights and justice – and what more it may be if only he endures…"

"One mirror of six. Five will remain."

"Already civil war looms, threatens to destroy everything that Haroun al-Rashid has built. Greedy princes and ambitious wizards position themselves to seize the kingdom. Thief-lords plot to ravage and loot. Our enemies gather to fall on us like wolves. The Caliph *must* be healed. One evil spirit should not be allowed to cause such devastation!"

The Rawun raised her hand. "All this is known, Sinbad the Sailor. All this was known before ever your wager was made. For us it is all part of the spectacle. Abu Mūsā Jābir ibn Hayyān is clever but we are the Children of Fire, the burning in the imagination, the genius of creation. We will save your Caliph, but at a price. You must make a decision."

"Not that one," begged Sinbad.

The wise woman of the Djinn indicated the silver mirrors. "Faithful Omar? Swashbuckling Henri? Fearless Ralf? Scholarly Rafi? Eager Haroun? Tormented Tishimi? Which shall it be?"

"Me!" cried Sinbad. "Let it be me! I'll die whatever miserable end you have for me. Do it, only save the Caliph and save Persia!"

The Rawun shook her head. "Fate is not done with you yet, Sinbad the Sailor. Your voyage must go on. If you would find the Court of the Djinn, plead your case to the Grand Sultan of Flame and Passion, recruit his aid to defeat this pale carrion-jinn that preys upon your monarch, then you must make a choice."

Sinbad slumped to his knees. "If you watched those mirrors then you already know my choice. You saw how much it took to teach me what I know now, how hard a path I traveled to become a man I can look at in a glass. You know I can never sacrifice any of them, and never will."

"Then you will never reach the Court of the Djinn."

Sinbad bowed his head. "So be it. I'll save Haroun al-Rashid some other way. Somehow."

"That is your decision?"

"That is my choice."

The Rawun reached down and stroked the sailor's cheek. "Foolish and sentimental and very human," she commented. She pressed into his hand a rich silver amulet set with a perfect sapphire. "The Test is not over. At your word this jewel will transport its wearer back here, to this Catacomb of Mirrors, to me. You have made your choice once, here, now. Can you sustain it as the hours of your Caliph's life ebb away, as all hope fails, as your civilization teeters on the brink of destruction? Or will you falter and return to choose again?"

Sinbad did not reply.

Neither Sinbad nor his crew could say how they awoke on the Blue Nymph a mere half-day's sailing from Basra. They trimmed their sail and returned home by night, avoiding the attention that would otherwise have overwhelmed the victors of the great race. Geber's green fire still plumed from the tower of the Thaumaturge's Guild, a beacon to draw them home.

"But we failed," Omar mourned. "All that for nothing! Why won't you tell us why you wouldn't enter the Djinn Court, Sinbad?"

"It's not important," the sailor answered. "All of you need to make ready for another voyage."

"What, now?" Henri asked in an exasperated voice. "Some of us have winnings to collect, you know."

"You are planning something, Captain Sinbad," Tishimi guessed. "What is it?"

"Well, I have one last idea to help the Caliph. I'll need to talk to Sage Geber again. But after that we may need to leave Baghdad in a hurry."

"Again," added Rafi.

The reports on the streets of Baghdad were not good. Haroun al-Rashid's health had declined; all now expected the Caliph's life to fail in the next few days. Many talked of a Ghul's curse, but no prayer or magic had been able to lift it.

Sinbad was almost at Geber's library when the thieves melted out of the shadows. The sailor recognized them at once as Ra's al Ŝâlouk's men. "You don't want me, boys," he told them. "I bring back too many rich cargoes for your master."

"You are exactly who we want, Sinbad," said the prince of scoundrels himself, emerging of the shadows behind his men. "I lost a lot of money wagering on that race of yours, and I am displeased with the outcome."

"You should know better than to bet against me," Sinbad cautioned. He calculated the odds right now and didn't like them.

"However unhappy I was, though, is nothing compared to the chagrin of Anwar abd Anwar," Ra's went on. "Yes, he lives. His temper is not improved by the loss of his wonderful air-boat nor the irreplaceable magics he had to expend to survive your tempest. It was he who promised me such a vast sum to accomplish your miserable end."

"I call that being a bad loser. You shouldn't have anything to do with men like that, Ra's."

The thief-lord chuckled. "I've always liked you, Sinbad – but I like gold more."

"I hear you've been taking more paupers into slavery."

"Do you have more treasure to redeem them before you die?"

"No. I'll have to free them some other way this time."

"Before you are slaughtered and I take your head to the Clockwork Sorcerer?"

Sinbad grinned like a tiger. "Think very carefully before you bet against me one last time, Ra's al Ŝâlouk."

The master-rogue sneered. "I'll take my chances." He gestured to his men. "Cut the sailor's throat."

The first two bravos to come at Sinbad fell with Henri's arrows in their backs. Sinbad whirled out his scimitar and sliced the third one across the neck.

A throaty roar came from the alleyway behind. The thugs lurking there were surprised when a giant blonde Norseman with a berserker axe fell upon them. Tishimi Osara sprang from the library's shadows to deal death to assassins who were not prepared for her intense, precise swordsmanship.

"Take them!" Ra's bellowed. "Take them all!" He was not afraid that the noise would call the watch. The guard had been well bribed to stay away.

Another flight of arrows toppled the thief archers on the rooftops. Henri rolled aside as a rattle of shafts clattered on the ledge where he had been and came up in a kneeling position to return fire again.

Sinbad danced back, shaking off the thieves who tried to grapple him. He fought with scimitar and dagger, pushing through the surprised and uncoordinated thugs straight towards Ra's al Sâlouk. The prince of scoundrels drew his own blade and hastily made ready to face the man he'd tried to murder.

Ralf had cleared the alleyway. He burst out into the square, scattering opponents, shouting insults and challenges in his blunt native tongue. Tishimi got his back, deftly fending off assassins who tried to flank them, darting with lethal precision when she saw opportunity.

"What's wrong, Ra's?" Sinbad challenged the thief-lord. "Did you really think I'm as dumb as I look?" He clattered through the last of the bravos and came at his foe.

Ra's al Sâlouk saw his men cut down "We don't have to fight," he told the sailor. "This is all a misunderstanding."

"I warned you I'd free the slaves, Ra's. I was pretty clear about it."

"They're released. I'll throw their chains off myself."

"No. This time it needs a longer-term solution," Sinbad pronounced. "You're fighting for your life, Ra's."

The prince of scoundrels' face colored with rage and he pressed forward. "Then die!" he cried.

Sinbad ran his blade through Ra's chest. "I'm told on pretty good authority that fate hasn't finished with me yet," he confided.

The remaining thieves scattered.

Henri dropped down from the rooftops. "Well that was a satisfying night's exercise," he admitted as he began checking money purses and gathering weapons.

"This thief was without honor," Tishimi declared. "His death was deserved. Now his victims will be free."

"Shall we go beat up that Anwar abd Anwar next?" Ralf offered.

"Maybe later," Sinbad grinned. "Right now I've got an appointment with…" His hand suddenly went to his throat and his smile vanished. "The Rawun's amulet! Someone must have grabbed it from me in the melee! It's gone!"

"The thief sold the amulet to the wine merchant," Sinbad explained to the beauteous Ayisha, "The merchant gave it to his wife. His wife returned it to me – in exchange for certain courtesies. Then the merchant came home and I had to depart rapidly." He gestured to himself. "And here I am."

"Here you are," agreed the princess, and kissed him again. Her soft arms embraced Sinbad, promising pleasures to come.

"So you retrieved the Rawun's amulet," Ayisha said at last, as they both recovered their breath from their passionate embrace. "My father's life is near its end. Do you intend to use the jewel to return to the Catacomb of Mirrors, to sacrifice one of your friends and save the kingdom?"

Sinbad shook his head. "That whole Test was a trap. The djinn promised that I'd be admitted to their court to plead my case. They never said the Sultan would grant me the means of saving Haroun al-Rashid. I'd murder one of my friends for no gain at all, save the laughter of the djinn."

"So the Caliph must die?"

"Not necessarily. You could save him, Ayisha."

The princess gave Sinbad a skeptical look. "And what is it I must do for you to save the Caliph, lustful adventurer?"

"You could just take the curse off him," the sailor suggested. "The one you placed there."

Ayisha sat up. "Why would you make such wild accusations?"

"Geber told me that the necromancies required to kill a Caliph must be renewed every day, but few people are permitted into Haroun's presence now. His beloved daughter is one of them. But what true daughter would flirt and hear vagabond stories while her father lay on his death bed?" Sinbad stroked his chin. "They say that Ghuls are clever shapeshifters. What became of the real Caliph of Baghdad's daughter, I wonder?"

Ayisha's pretty face twisted. "Gone where none will find her," she promised. "None will find you either, Sinbad the Sailor. I shall enjoy devouring you. It is a pity I could not take more pleasure of you first."

The Ghul rose and shifted to her rotted twisted true-self. Sinbad scrabbled away from the bed, but he was weaponless save for the twin knives he'd used to climb to the window.

"Release the Caliph," Sinbad asked the Ghul. "Please. If you go back to your other shape we could even continue our date."

"You are an idiot, Sinbad the Sailor. You kissed me. Now you cannot harm me, and must obey me in all things."

"A lot of folks have called me idiot and fool recently," Sinbad remembered. "And yet I'm still here. And now I'll save the Caliph."

"How?" scorned the Ghul.

"I'll make a choice, of course. The Rawun gave me an amulet that would return the wearer to her when I spoke the word. While you and I were kissing I fastened it on you."

The Ghul's hands flew to her neck. The delicate silver chain with the glowing sapphire was locked there.

"I told you the whole thing was a trap," Sinbad said. And he commanded the gem to return to the Sapphire Isle.

The Ghul screamed once as she realized she'd been tricked, and then she was whisked away to face the judgment of the Rawun.

In his suite downstairs, Haroun al Rashid opened his eyes and recognized his attendants. The spell on the Caliph was broken.

Sinbad finished his wine, then lowered himself from the princess' tower the same way that he'd come.

Geber awaited Sinbad in the deserted marketplace at the base of the palace wall. "All is well," the Sage told the sailor. "Except…"

"Except what?" Sinbad felt that he deserved at least the rest of the night off.

"Except the Princess Ayisha is missing. The real Caliph of Baghdad's daughter."

"Sounds like a good problem for someone else."

"You'd think so, wouldn't you?" the greatest Sage of Persia smiled sympathetically. "I'll let you know when the time comes for you to seek her."

"Oh, good." Sinbad turned away. "Farewell, Geber. I need to be gone before the wine merchant gets to the assassins guilds, or the Clockwork Sorcerer winds up more of his toys, or the new master-rogue starts up a vendetta, or anyone asks what happened to the Princess of Persia. I'm thinking a nice, long, distant sea voyage, starting very soon. Maybe tonight!"

"Good seas, then, and fine adventures." The old Sage stroked his beard and watched Sinbad go. The young traveler had so many miles to go. The djinn's traps for that young man had scarcely begun.

But Geber would bet on Sinbad the Sailor!

The End

Pulping Sinbad

Those who feel that pulp fiction can only be about 30s detectives helping shady dames and dodging gat-wielding goons misunderstand the genre. Pulp's roots run deep. Pulp traces its lineage to popular stories that thrilled common people back as far as mythology. Fast paced, action driven, pulse-pounding, mind-blowing tales of heroes like Robin Hood or Hercules are as much in the domain of pulp as Sam Spade or the Shadow.

One such ancestor is A Thousand Nights and a Night, the assembled corpus of Middle Eastern and South Asian stories from Islam's "golden age". This great work of folklore, set in the brief and shining Caliphate Era of the 8th century, impacted on the Western world during Victorian times and popularised stories such as Ali Baba and the Forty Thieves, Aladdin and his Lamp, and of course The Voyages of Sinbad the Sailor. Equally famous was the tales' narrator, the maritally-challenged Scheherazade, a young lady who came up with a most unique solution to an unfair divorce settlement.

The Thousand Nights is a story about stories. Scheherazade entertains her Caliph husband nightly with a tale told to her sister, and the cliffhanger ending each morning prevents him from having her executed like his previous wives. Surely no pulp writer has ever had better incentive to keep her stories compelling, engaging, or visceral, or to leave her audience desperate for the next chapter?

There are stories within her stories too. Often a protagonist in Scheherazade's accounts tells his own tale to some other character - and that story might include reports of an adventure yet another person might have told him. Stories within stories within stories, with us as the final listener to all of them! Sinbad's voyages are told in this manner, as the Sailor describes his fortunes and misfortunes to a beggar at his door.

Sinbad's exploits follow one of the three great story-forms as defined by Robert A. Heinlein. It is true that in Sinbad's tales Boy Meets Girl (Sinbad is married at least twice) and that A Man Learns A Lesson (Sinbad makes and learns from mistakes), but overwhelmingly he is that Man Who Goes On a Journey. He is of that great tradition of explorer-adventurers that stretches back to Jason and Odysseus and reaches forward to James T. Kirk and Doctor Who. Sinbad sails.

Pulp literature is full of voyages of discovery, as far back as Verne's "Voyage to the Centre of the Earth" and H.G. Wells' "The First Men on the Moon". So it feels right to reclaim Sinbad and send him out discovering new places – and new trouble – for the new pulp age.

Being a traditionalist I encourage my fellow authors not to throw out anything that gave the original stories their flavour. The Arabian Nights tales were action-filled, raunchy, sometimes brutal, often magical. They were set in an idealised, fictionalised world centred around a Baghdad as mythical as Camelot, populated by enough monsters to keep Ray Harryhausen happy for life. Any voyage of Sinbad that attempts to make him a social-working philosopher in a realistic setting where magic is mere superstition is doomed to fail.

Sinbad the Sailor is also Sinbad the Fast-Talking Trader, Sinbad the Swashbuckler, Sinbad the Ladies Man, and Sinbad the Survivor. He's the man who can be carried off to a Roc's nest to be devoured and get home with pockets full of diamonds. He's sentenced to execution by a tyrant king one moment and he's fleeing from demons with a princess in tow the next. For Sinbad there is always another horizon, another shore, another deal, another story.

Revisiting old tales for inspiration offers the opportunity to use modern techniques to tell new stories about classic characters. Contemporary audiences expect clear motivations and more description of places and situations. We are now a society of readers and viewers who demand detail, character, and backstory as prerequisites for suspension of disbelief. We're literate in cutscenes, foreshadowing, and internal monologues. Hence the version of Sinbad in this volume has been furnished with a supporting cast, an extraordinary ship, and a fleshed out world, the better to meet the requirements of modern storytelling.

And with Sinbad it always comes back to the stories and to the voyages. Get those right and the rest follows naturally.

For my contribution to this volume I knew I wanted a story within a story, this time with Sinbad himself providing the framing sequence for the course of events. But I also wanted to bring the conclusion right into Sinbad's narration, revealing that what readers thought was a framing conceit was actually an integral part of the plot all along. I wanted the story to dip back into 'previous' stories (all drawn either from Scheherazade's accounts or from editor Ron Fortier's character guide-notes) to offer the layered tale-spinning that is characteristic of the milieu. I wanted to send Sinbad off the map to somewhere new and strange, then I wanted that strangeness to come home with him. And I wanted to do all of this within an adventure story that ticked all the reader's expectations of rooftop chases, beautiful princesses, wizards, monsters, and genuine heroism.

So I chewed it all up together and spat out a wad of writing that blended all those aspirations into a single story mass. The stuff that's made when you do that? It's called pulp.

I.A. Watson - enjoys telling stories but hates writing paragraphs about himself for pages like this one. He nurses his compulsive writing habits with the help of occasional novels such as his award-nominated *Robin Hood: King of Sherwood* and *Robin Hood: Arrow of Justice* and *Blackthorn: Dynasty of Mars* or by contributing stories to anthologies such as *Sherlock Holmes: Consulting Detective* volumes 1-3, *Gideon Cane - Demon Hunter, The New Adventures of Richard Knight, Blackthorn - Thunder On Mars, Blood-Price of the Missionary's Gold* and *Sentinels: Alternate Visions.* A full list of his publications, free samples, and some complete short stories are available at http://www.chillwater.org.uk/writing/

SINBAD & the VOYAGE to the LAND of the FROZEN SUN

by
Derrick Ferguson

And in the evening when the sun set on Baghdad, greatest city of the world and dusky fingers of twilight darkened into full night, men betook themselves to the taverns, inns and gambling houses to spend their time in fellowship and good talk, fueled with much wine, song and laughter. And there was no finer tavern to be found in all of Baghdad than that known all throughout the city as The Great Hall of Cups.

Operated by old Abu Ironseeker himself, in years long since passed he had been the very terror of all the Seven Seas and when it was heard that he was out and about on his ship, The Dragon's Curse, it was the wise captain that kept his ship in port until he knew of the exact whereabouts of Abu Ironseeker. Unlike most of his now deceased brethren of The Pirate Brotherhood (May Allah the Merciful have compassion on their black souls!) Abu had enough sense to know when to give up the trade of piracy. He retired to Baghdad, married a lusty woman with a disposition to match her ample behind and generous bosom, opened The Great Hall of Cups and considered himself the most fortunate and wisest of men.

A robust and lively place this, The Great Hall of Cups. Nine enormous fireplaces kept the establishment warm and toasty. Pigs and huge slabs of beef or long spits with a dozen chickens roasted in all of them. The common room was lit as brightly as noontime in the Market Square by huge bronze chandeliers that Abu swore on his grandfather's beard he had himself looted from the palace of the Emir of Daibul. The serving wenches served with a will and wicked smiles. And they were as adept at balancing huge platters of food and drink as well as in avoiding the wandering hands of their customers.

And what customers! Rogues, adventurers, pirates, mercenaries, sailors, soldiers, wanderers from all corners of the wild, wide world. Many of them legends in their own right in their own far lands and distant cities. But soon or late, all made their way to Baghdad. For it was a city of legends. No, it was more than that; far more. It was THE city of legends.

Flame haired Shireen, the most beautiful and sensual dancer in all of Baghdad danced on a wooden table as large and as wide as the wheel of the caliph's own magnificent carriage. Her shameless smile and licentious eyes bespoke of pleasures that only a real woman could provide. Even over the shouts, curses, songs and stories of the dozens of men packed into the tavern, the music she wantonly danced to could be heard. It sounded clear and sweet even over the general clamor. No one minded the smells, the sweat, and the noise. It was all sounds of life. Sweet, sweet life.

Over in the center of the room, surrounded by an audience who hooted and cast bawdy jests whenever they deemed appropriate, Jamel Dreadbeard held court as usual. A man of immense size and appetites was Jamel Dreadbeard. And so were the stories he told. His raging voice, as ragged as that of tearing sail cloth rebounded from the great smoke-blackened wooden roof beams as he finished his story;

"And I swear in the name of The Prophet that we were pursued by the Shenlong for three days and three nights! It deluged us with constant wind and rain that we fought as if it were a thing alive!" Jamel Dreadbeard thumped his hairy chest with a fist as big as a ham. "Lashed meself to me own wheel I did! Had no choice if we were going to make it back to port!"

"What happened to the treasure you stole from the Tomb of Twilight?" a derisive voice asked. A voice that plainly indicated its owner had heard this story before and knew how it ended but just couldn't resist twisting the knife in a bit.

"May Allah rot thy liver! Thou knowest full well that I had to order my men to throw it overboard to lighten the ship so that we would not sink as we sailed through The Boiling Sea!"

Another voice sang out boisterously, "And what of the Chinese princess you kidnapped from The City of The Nine Rings?"

"And I curse thee for a humorless clod! Thou too know that the Shenlong reclaimed the princess to restore her to her throne. My crew and I were lucky to escape with our lives."

Yet another voice spoke up. But this one was from the entrance. It was a voice full of humor and controlled power. It was a voice made for the open sea where its owner did not have to keep it in check. "So off you go on this grand quest but you lose the treasure, you lose the princess and you get chased home by a mischievous spirit who makes it rain a bit! Bah! And you call yourself an adventurer!"

All knew the voice well and they turned with shouts and cheers of welcome on their lips, holding up their flagons or wine and rum in salute.

The man, who stood framed in the circular open doorway with his fists on his hips, threw back his head and let out with a laugh that filled the tavern. The night wind billowed the blood-red silk crimson cloak he wore. The wooden grip of a scimitar sheathed on his back could be seen behind his left shoulder where he could get at it most easily. But if not, the throwing knife in the ornamented scabbard thrust into the wide crimson Bakhariot sash about his waist would do. The silk sky blue shirt matched his turban. His embroidered baggy sailor's pants and Kurdish boots were handmade and of the finest quality to be had.

A handsome rogue, this one, standing there bold as a peacock as if escaped from The Devil's own clutches. His wonderfully dark skin and dark blue eyes the benefit of his mixed Moorish and Nubian bloods. Of average height, the first impression one had of him was that of slimness. It was a deceptive impression. So well molded was he that one would not suspect his body combined the strength of a lion and the steel trap swiftness of a panther. His face he kept meticulously clean shaven, save for his beard and mustache which he trimmed himself nearly every day for he was fond of it and had been ever since the Princess Parisa had told him it gave a delightfully sinister cast to his features.

"Sinbad! Sinbad! SINBAD!"

Sinbad bowed graciously and joined his friends at Jamel Dreadbeard's table, sweeping off his cloak as grandly as if he were in the Caliph's palace instead of a tavern. Shireen, upon spying Sinbad, leapt from the table and dashed over to spring into his arms.

"Sinbad! Where have you been? It has been long since you've spent your nights here!"

Sinbad kissed her warmly and patted her desirable bottom. "Ah, my dove, did you think I did not miss your embraces or the laughter of my good friends here? But I am a sailor and the sea is my true love. While she may let me stray once in a while into the arms of a woman of flesh and blood, she always calls me back."

"And I suppose that you have yet another tale of your adventures to tell us?" Jamel Dreadbeard grumbled.

"One considerably better than yours, I assure you," Sinbad replied, waving for a serving wench to bring him wine. He clapped one of the seated men on the back. "Melik, do you not tire of hearing Jamel's same old story? I swear I must have heard it ten times already!"

"Not all of us can be the illustrious Sinbad! The prince of sailors, the master of adventure!" Jamel Dreadbeard muttered as he sat down for he knew from long experience that he was about to lose his audience.

"'Tis true, 'tis true," Sinbad said with mock humility. The light seemed to sparkle on his wide smile. "But your fault, friend Dreadbeard is that your adventures never end with you any richer or wiser than when you began."

"Unlike you! Doubtless you have returned from yet another voyage?"

Sinbad took a long swallow from his tankard before replying, "You speak with the tongue of a prophet and do not know it! I have just returned a mere few days ago from a voyage to fabled Cobophia itself!"

As if by the blackest of magic, the entire tavern fell silent. Sinbad's voice carried far and carried loud due to years of shouting orders at sea and his words had been plainly heard by those close to him and those who hadn't were quickly apprised of what he had said by those who had not. Sinbad looked around innocently. "Did I utter wrongly?"

It was Yusuf the Seven-Fingered who answered for them all. "You did indeed, O boastful one! You are many things, Sinbad El Ari, but none here would ever have counted a liar among them!"

Sinbad's blue eyes flashed wrathfully like twin stars. "You dare call Sinbad a liar to his face?"

"Aye! And again I call thee liar!"

"You and I have broken bread and sailed together many times, Yusef. Why do you insult a true friend such as I to his face?"

"Because none have ever returned from the land of The Frozen Sun in their right mind as thou knowest full well, Sinbad! Thrice I call thee liar! And aye, again I shall if you persist!"

"Did I lie when I returned with the tale of my voyage to the fabled land of Deryabar where I found the treasure of Alexander the Great? You there, Aga the One-Eyed! You shall answer for me! Did I lie then?"

"No, Sinbad, you did not! I swear by my plucked-out eye!"

Sinbad grunted in satisfaction and turned to another man, "Moga! You remember when I returned from my voyage to the isle of Colossa! Was that a lie?"

"Indeed it was not, Sinbad."

"Nor were my voyages to Lemuria or Hyperboria or a dozen other lands that are fabled in song and story! I, Sinbad have been to all of them and brought back proof that backs up my words. So why should you disbelieve me now when I say I have been to Cobophia?"

"Because Cobophia is the land where time does not exist. It is the Land of The Frozen Sun. What mind of mortal man can stay sane in a land where there is no time?"

"You can close thy thoughts and remain forever in bewilderment, O son of ignorance. Or you can give ear and grow in wisdom and enlightenment. Which shall it be?"

The shouts of cries of "Tell us! Tell us!" filled the tavern. And Sinbad need no more urging than that. As lightly as sea foam he leaped upon the table and spread his arms wide, the light flashing from his ornate golden wristbands.

"Gather 'round, then, O Masters! Come closer and listen to my tale most wondrous and strange! Fill the cups and tankards of my brothers, fair ones! For they will need thy strong drink as they hear of Sinbad's voyage to Cobophia, The Land of The Frozen Sun! Know me O Sons of Allah for the truth of my words. And by the ears of The Prophet, every word I speak is true!"

"Say on, Sinbad!"

"My story begins in Basra, my brothers. My crew and I had sailed to the Isle of Dawn to pick up a most precious cargo for the learned philosophers of Basra. Scrolls and books from many different corners of the world. These were documents they paid most handsomely for. And it was while my ship, The Blue Nymph was being unloaded that..."

❀ ❀ ❀

The knock on the door of Sinbad's quarters was most insistent and a knock that he knew well. Curiously, all of Sinbad's trusted friends had a different way of knocking on his door and he knew them as well as he knew their voices and their footsteps. "Enter, Tishimi!"

The door opened and Tishimi Osara came into the richly decorated quarters of her captain. 'Richly' was the politest way Tishimi would have put it if pressed to describe her captain's quarters. But in her private thoughts, 'hedonistic' or even 'decadent' would have been a more honest description. A lithe six inches over five feet, Tishimi's breathtaking beauty deceptively hid her dangerous nature. Just by looking at her in her quiet black silk clothing none would suspect her of being a samurai. But she would not be a full member of Sinbad's crew if she could not hold her own.

Sinbad sat at his baroque carved table of decorative ebony, looking at his charts, a jeweled goblet of good Basran wine close at hand. "Come in, come in," Sinbad waved her over. "I am planning our next trip. Muallin the wine merchant has a shipment he needs to get to the kingdom of Chandra in time for their Satrap's birthday celebration. Not very exciting but Muallin is a friend and the crew can take shore leave at the celebration." Sinbad looked up. His typical roguish demeanor was not in evidence. Which was usual when he conducted his ship's business or when one of his friends looked so serious. "Is aught amiss, Tishimi?"

"I merely wish to ask a favor, Sinbad."

"This does sound serious," Sinbad said, gesturing for her to sit. He did not ask if she would partake of wine. Tishimi did not drink socially, only on special occasions. And Tishimi did not ask favors of any man or woman. "What favor may I grant? Ask and it shall be done."

"The cargo of scrolls and books. I was assisting with the unloading and I spied a book that I would like very much to own. I do not ask you make a gift of it. I will pay."

Sinbad waved his hand, the gold wristband sparkling. "I shall not hear of it. You may take any book or scroll you wish. The philosophers of Basra will not miss it. And if they do, I shall deal with the matter. Think no more on it. What book is this?"

"One written by a man named Sun Tzu. A book on the strategy and philosophy of war. I was most surprised to see it as I believed that there were no copies of this book outside of Asia."

"I would be interested to read this book myself."

"There is much you can learn from it. Once I have read it I should be honored to lend it to you if you promise that we discuss it afterwards."

"Of course. I.." Again there was insistent knocking at his door. And again, he bade the knocker to come in.

This time it was Haroun, his wild curly dark hair framing his young face. "Captain Sinbad, Omar requests you come on deck. Someone wishes to see you."

Sinbad pushed himself out of his chair and followed by Haroun and Tishimi made his way to the deck of The Blue Nymph. The hot afternoon sun struck brilliant fire from the spires and minarets of Basra. The wharfs and docks were as always a circus of controlled chaos with ships being loaded and unloaded, sailors cursing and singing as they went about their work. Beggars begged, whores strutted to and fro, children excitedly dashed to and fro on errands for the sailors or their captains. Merchants pushed their carts themselves or had them pulled by donkeys.

Omar stood by the gangplank, looking down at the dock. A compact mass of muscle was Omar. Still young for a sailor, despite his graying beard and hair. An orphan, Omar had shipped out as a cabin boy and from then on, the sea was his life. He and Sinbad met when they both sailed with the Sindh, the best sailors in the world. When Sinbad became the owner of The Blue Nymph he at once sought out Omar and brought him onboard as his First Mate. In many ways it was actually Omar who ran The Blue Nymph.

"What troubles thee, Master Omar that you must need summon me from my maps?" Despite the sternness in his voice, the twinkle in his blue eyes and the friendly slap on the back told Omar that Sinbad was glad for any distraction that would bring him out into the sunlight and fresh air.

"There are two ladies asking to see you, Captain." Omar jerked his head at the ladies in question.

The one whose Sinbad's gaze landed on first was a twisted old woman who looked to be about a hundred years old. Her pure white hair so stringy and thin that she might as well have plucked the strands from her liver spotted scalp and gone bald. Her robes were of good quality, however and the ornately carved stick that aided her to stand and walk looked to Sinbad to be of good Kihoaok wood. That wood was very expense and very difficult to carve. Her sunken gray eyes belied the age of her limbs, however. They were eyes as sharp and as cunning as those of a lynx.

But her companion...now she was another matter altogether...of athletic build that bespoke of many hours of hard work, this was no pampered house servant despite her modest garments. The swell of her bosom, the roundness of hip and long tanned legs were enough to give pause to any man worthy to call himself such. Straight silky platinum hair hung down to what surely had to be magnificently shaped buttocks, Sinbad reckoned. She looked up at him silently with eyes of pewter.

"And why do you have such noble ladies waiting, Master Omar? You do not invite them onboard to enjoy the hospitality of our fine ship?"

"By your own orders, Captain Sinbad, none may board The Blue Nymph while cargo is being loaded or unloaded. I merely enforce thy will."

Sinbad ignored Omar. Sometimes it was best that way. Sinbad knew full well why Omar hadn't invited them on board. A staunch traditionalist, he believed that women had no place on a ship. Of course, when he met up with Tishimi he had to modify that attitude somewhat. Especially when he learned she had saved Sinbad's life from assassins. From then on, Omar had taken her side and kept the crew in line, some of whom still grumbled about having a woman on board. However, they well knew her skill with her katana and tanto and let her be. But Omar's acceptance of Tishimi did not extend to other women.

"Ladies!" Sinbad called down. "You seek Sinbad?"

"We do," the crone answered in a surprisingly strong voice more suited to a woman half her age. "May we come aboard, captain? We have a business proposition to discuss."

"Come aboard and be welcome, old mother."

The old woman and her companion started up the gangplank but the thunderous sounds of silver shod horses hooves on cobblestones gave them pause. Sinbad turned to look as well.

Coming down the dock were a dozen wild-eyed riders, their striped crimson and black cloaks flapping around them. Their huge black horses snorted and huffed as they hurtled through the crowds on the dock, not caring who or what was in their way. Men and women cursed and yelled as they dived into doorways or under wagons for cover, leaped into the water or fled shrieking into narrow alleyways as the reckless riders came to a stop. Their leader pointed at the old woman. "Not another step, old crow! You come with us!" The men behind him drew their swords as one. Fierce looking warriors they were, glaring at Sinbad with savage eyes under heavy brows.

"And who might you be, fellow?"

The leader looked up at Sinbad. His luxurious black hair stood up and away from his large head like the quills of a porcupine. His skin was almost as dark as Sinbad's but his eyes were inky and burned with rage. Judging by the huge scimitar scabbarded on his saddle he was a man of considerable strength. "I am Bavathi The Executioner. I am here on the business of The Priestess of Moonsilver Keep. Tend to thy business and I will do likewise."

"Well, I do believe that this is my business, friend." Sinbad's voice rang out jovially as he started down the gangplank. "This old woman and her delightful companion have asked for the hospitality of my ship and I have given it. That makes them my guests and under my protection. State your grievance with the old one or be off with you."

Bavathi's eyes became darker and even more intense, if such was possible. He struggled to control his horse. The animal's blood was hot from the run and standing in one spot was not to its liking. "I have given you my name. Should you not do likewise?"

"A thousand pardons, my friend! I am Sinbad El Ari, captain of this fine

"And who might you be, fellow?"

vessel named The Blue Nymph. Peace, mercy and Allah's blessings on you." Sinbad said, raising the fingers of his right hand to his lips and then to his forehead with a flourish.

Custom demanded that Bavathi reply with a better greeting but instead his response was; "I have heard of you. Men say you make it your occupation to meddle in affairs that do not concern you. Such as our present situation. I say again, the women come with me. And here are swords aplenty at my back to enforce my word."

"And I have this to enforce mine." Sinbad placed pinkies in the corners of his mouth and let out with a peculiar, undulating whistle. And his answer was in the form of an ear-shattering barbaric yell. Pounding feet were heard coming up a flight of stairs from below decks and a bearded blond giant appeared at the top of the gangplank. His long ponytail whipped about madly as his head turned this way and that. Armored all in leather, in his massive right hand he held a broadsword of fearsome length. And just as fearsome was the ten pound double-edged battle axe in the left hand. Sinbad grinned at the expression on the faces of Bavathi's men. It was rare indeed in this part of the world to see a Viking warrior. And upon seeing one for the first time as these men were doing was enough to give even battle seasoned warriors such as they pause.

"Who dares give insult to my sword brother Sinbad?" the blond giant demanded. Sinbad merely pointed at Bavathi and his men. With a bellow that made the horses whinny in terror, the Viking leaped from the deck of the Blue Nymph in a tremendous bound that seemed impossible for one of his size. He landed in the middle of the riders and the red carnage began. Sinbad rapped out quick orders to Omar; "Get these women on board and below decks! Somebody throw me a sword!"

And just that quickly, one of his loyal sailors tossed him a scimitar. The Viking had already downed three of the riders and they lay on the cobbles, their blood spurting from terrible wounds. The broadsword and axe were such destructive weapons that powered by the immense thews of the Viking, only a single stroke was needed from each to do damage.

Sinbad himself leaped in front of Bavathi's horse. "Come down from there so that I may teach you the proper respect for your betters, my friend!"

Bavathi's hand reached down for his great scimitar but before he could draw it, an arrow thudded into the thick leather saddle right next to next to the grip of the scimitar, causing Bavathi to draw back the hand in surprise. The arrow did not pierce the saddle to injure the horse but the shock of the arrow's impact was enough to cause the horse to rear, legs flailing wildly.

With a curse Bavathi fell off backward, tumbling arse over heels.

Sinbad looked over his shoulder at the bored looking archer who lay in the curve of the ship's prow. He had made the shot from his reclining position as easily as if he did it every day. "You robbed me of teaching this fellow manners, Henri!"

Henri Delacroix yawned. "Take your brawling elsewhere, then. I was sleeping here and not troubling a soul when you and that barbarian oaf started your infernal fighting."

Omar couldn't help but put in, "You should do your sleeping in your quarters, then. Men work up here on deck."

The Gaul yawned again, more exaggerated this time and said, "You would do well to cease chiding me and tend to watching Sinbad's back," he gestured in Sinbad's direction.

Indeed, Bavathi had gotten to his feet and drawn his scimitar. A veritable fan of shining steel it was. Thrice as broad as any scimitar Sinbad had ever seen and next to that weapon, the scimitar in his hand looked as formidable as a toothpick. He wished he had his own scimitar, fabricated for him by The Masters of The White Forge. But his favored weapon was in his quarters. Still, Sinbad's heart had never failed in a fight and so he prepared himself for battle.

But it was not to be so. More clattering of hooves as the Sultan of Basra's own bodyguards, The Steel Leopards stormed into the middle of the brawl, encircling Bavathi's men with their weapons. The Viking bellowed at them; "Find your own! These dogs belong to me!"

Bavathi broke off and dashed for his horse, vaulted into the saddle. He wheeled his animal about to depart but threw last words over his shoulder; "Be sure that this is not over between us, Sinbad El Ari. Only your head upon a pike will satisfy me." And then he was away, the remnants of his men following as they galloped away with Sinbad's mocking laughter in their ears.

The Viking glowered at the Steel Leopards in their ornate steel armor. At his feet lay six men, two of them near cloven in half by that terrible axe. One man still lived although it was only by Allah's true mercy. His left side was a red ruin from where The Viking's backhand sword stroke had caught him. Only the jazerant he wore underneath the black and red robes had saved him from immediate death. The Viking roared and lifted his sword to finish him off.

"Ralf! Stay thy hand!"

Only the command of Sinbad prevented that sword from finishing its bloody job. Ralf Gunarson stepped away from the cowering man, his frosty blue eyes full of bloodlust. "He is yours, Sinbad. But by Odin's Spear, I see not the sense in letting a foe live."

"I suspect he has much to tell us. As do the women and my friend Sokurah. Hail, Commander of the Steel Leopards! You do us much honor with your assistance."

Ralf Gunarson grunted and muttered as Sinbad stepped over the rescued victim; "I needed no assistance."

Sinbad embraced the Commander of The Steel Leopards. Sokurah stood nearly a head taller than Sinbad. Sokurah had been a sailor himself, joining Sinbad on a number of voyages until an adventure where Sinbad had saved the life of the Sultan's ninth wife. It was during that adventure Sokurah fell in love with the Sultan's fourth wife. So grateful was the Sultan he honored Sinbad's request to divorce his fourth wife that she could marry Sokurah. It was the Sultan's own idea to make Sokurah commander of his bodyguards and it was a decision all concerned never regretted.

"What is all this business, Sokurah? Who was that man and why does he pursue those women?"

"Those women were supposed to wait for me. The Sultan himself asked me to bring them to you. Sinbad, they need your help."

"Then come aboard, my friend so that we may talk in peace. Omar, you and Tishimi come with me. Sokurah, have two of your men bring that wounded dog on board. Haroun! Find Rafi and tell him to bring his medicines and poultices as he has a patient! Henri!"

The archer languidly raised himself up from where he lay. "Am I never to finish a decent nap aboard this ship of clamor and chaos?"

"Bestir your lazy hide and take over supervising the unloading! You sleep far too much for one so young."

"Cannot it wait until you or Omar are free?"

"It is written that the dogs may bark but the caravan moves on. To work, I say!"

Henri sighed and rolled off the curve of the prow to carry out his captain's orders. Ralf Gunarson had already found his work.

He gathered the bodies of the dead.

Sinbad waved at his table and indicated that everybody should find a seat as best as they could. Tishimi held out a chair for the old woman to sit and the younger woman smiled her thanks. She sat next to the old woman as did Tishimi. Sokurah gratefully removed his conical helmet that he was required to wear at all times while on duty. It looked impressive and intimidating, yes. But also hot. Sinbad remained standing, his arms folded across his muscular chest, never having taken his eyes off the old woman's companion. "We haven't even been properly introduced," he said. Omar, standing a little behind Sinbad scratched the side of his thick neck, a habit he had when he didn't like something. Omar tended to scratch his neck a lot.

It was Sokurah who did the introductions. "The old woman is Zenobia. Her companion is Farah. They are from Moonsilver Abbey, in the mountains above Basra."

"I have never heard of this abbey," Sinbad said, his words directed at Zenobia but his eyes never leaving the delicate face of Farah.

"We worship Rhysilis, she who is the Mother of The Phoenix," Zenobia said. "I have been the High Priestess of the abbey for nigh on sixty years now. But my loyal sisters were brutally and treacherously slain and I was forced to leave Moonsilver Abbey which has been my home for longer than I can remember."

"What happened?" Tishimi asked, placing her hand over the old woman's.

"A wretched wench who thinks far too much of herself usurped my authority. She seduced Bavathi and made use of his mercenaries to slay all who would not bend the knee to her. She declared herself Priestess and through her black arts learned the location of The Well of Apollo."

Sinbad turned his head to swap a look of mixed disbelief with amazement with Omar. Tishimi noticed the look as she tended to notice everything around her. "The Well of Apollo?"

"It is a well. But not of water." Sinbad replied thoughtfully. "It is said that the very lifeblood of the universe fills The Well of Apollo and he who bathes in its cosmic essence shall gain immortality."

"Bah. Stuff and nonsense. Tales sailors tell to amuse themselves on long voyages when they should be working." Omar said firmly.

"And how many lands and creatures have we encountered that were supposed to be stuff and nonsense, my friend?" Sinbad said. He turned back to Zenobia. "Say on, old mother. What has this to do with you and this sorceress?"

"Her name is Iskosia, may her indiscretions rot her liver! And for many years she pretended to be humble and the friendliest of my followers, all the while secretly practicing magic so black and so dangerous that that I shiver to think of what bargains she must have made with what demons to acquire the abilities she possesses." Zenobia gestured for Farah to pour her some wine, which she did. With her aged throat properly lubricated, Zenobia continued her story.

"Iskosia heard me tell of The Well of Apollo and attempted to wheedle and cajole the information out of me. But I would not tell. Such information is not for her or for any mortal!"

"Except for you, of course," Omar said sarcastically. Tishimi threw him a furious glare.

"What part do you play in this drama, my friend?" Sinbad asked Sokurah.

"The Sultan is concerned of what would happen if Iskosia gains such power. For many years he has been a friend to Moonsilver Abbey. But that was when Zenobia was Priestess. Already there are rumors of what Iskosia plans to do to extend her influence and power among the people of Basra."

"Then why does the Sultan not take this witch and hang her properly?" Omar demanded.

Sokurah spread his hands helplessly. "Alas, while our Sultan is the bravest of men when it comes to fighting human foes, his courage fails him when magic is mentioned."

Omar stepped forward. "I like not where this is going, Sinbad. We have business aplenty awaiting us in half a dozen ports and the trade routes will soon be crowded with competitors. We have no time for this."

"Hush, Omar." Sinbad waved a hand to further silence the sputtering first mate as he said, "And what is it that you wish of me, old mother?"

"The courage and daring of Sinbad and his crew are well known all throughout the world. I would hire you and your ship to take me to The Well of Apollo before Iskosia gets there and works her wickedness."

"And where is it?"

"Cobophia, The Land of The Frozen Sun."

"What?" Omar exclaimed. "Sinbad, this is madness! Cobophia is the land where time does not exist! It lies beyond The Sea of Jade Mist and those fortunate few who have returned were not whole in mind or body."

Sokurah spoke rapidly. "I speak for the Sultan, Sinbad. He promises three full chests of gold and the most precious jewels in his treasure house if you will take Priestess Zenobia and Farah to Cobophia."

"And once we get there, what are we to do?"

"Nothing," Zenobia said firmly. "Merely get me there and I shall do the rest."

"You may have five of my own Steel Leopards to assist you, Sinbad,"

Sokurah said. "I would go myself but my first duty is to my Sultan and I cannot take the chance that there would be assassins who would take advantage of my absence."

"Neither would I take you from your sworn duty, old friend. The company of your five good and stout Steel Leopards is more than enough. But there is one more thing I must ask."

"And what is that, Captain Sinbad?" Zenobia inquired.

"Not from you, old mother. Her." Sinbad gestured at Farah. "I would know what she thinks of this and what her wishes are."

Farah looked up and Sinbad felt his heart beat faster. He had known many beautiful women but Farah not only was extraordinarily beautiful, she had an innocence in her eyes that he found irresistibly attractive. She looked into his eyes and said with utter sincerity, "I go where Priestess Zenobia goes. I serve the will of The Mother of The Phoenix."

"The trip will be dangerous."

Farah bowed her head. "As the Mother wills."

Again, a knock at the door and young Haroun stuck his head in. "Captain? Rafi has tended to the wounds of the dog who fell under Ralf's sword."

"Can he talk?"

"Alas, he was not able to stomach the tender ministrations of our physician and passed out. Rafi claims he will be awake in a few hours."

"No matter. We will bring him with us. Haroun, five Steel Leopards will be joining us. You see to their care as long as they are on board."

"Aye, Captain. May I ask where we are going?"

"You will find out with the rest of the crew. Be off with you." Haroun closed the door and went about his work. Sinbad looked around the room. "It is settled, then. Sokurah, you may tell the Sultan I accept the task. The Blue Nymph sails with the morning tide."

"I thank you, Sinbad. My gratitude will be eternal."

"You and the Sultan have long been friends to myself and my crew. Is Sinbad an ungrateful wretch that he does not repay friendship?" Sinbad hugged Sokurah. "You will stay and dine with me this evening?"

"I should be delighted."

Sinbad nodded. "Tishimi, Priestess Zenobia and Farah I entrust to your care."

Zenobia said, "I thank you, Captain Sinbad. The Mother will bless you all your days."

"And Allah's blessings on you, old mother."

"We will all need Allah's blessings on this trip," Omar groused. "Sinbad, we have far better and more profitable things to do with our time than get involved in this pagan nonsense. Leave the old woman to go look for her heathen gods on her own!"

"Have you ever known me to refuse the request of a damsel in distress, Omar?"

"She has not been a damsel for more years than I care to think."

Sinbad's immense laughter boomed out once again. "Ah, Omar, what would I do without you? Go, assemble the crew on deck so that I might tell them of our new voyage!"

❀ ❀ ❀

Bavathi The Executioner stomped up the hundred quartz steps that led up and into Moonsilver Abbey. His mood, never pleasant even under the best of circumstances was now blacker than the floor of Hell itself. He stalked through the mosaic halls of the Abbey and none dared meet his eye or ask his business. It had long been the custom that men did not walk imperiously through the halls of Moonsilver Abbey unescorted. But these were now very different times.

He did not knock on the gilded double doors leading to the suite of rooms that had belonged to Zenobia but now were occupied by Iskosia the Usurper. He slammed them open and stalked through the rooms until reaching the one that contained a small heated pool of scented water for the private comfort of the Priestess. Bavathi entered and his voice was pure hatred as he snarled; "The wenches escaped me!"

The woman he spoke to ignored him. Bavathi stood there; hand on the grip of his great scimitar, trembling with anger. The woman did not swim in her pool alone. Dozens of snakes of different sizes swam with her, winding about her limbs, her torso. One of the snakes, a boa constrictor as thick around as Bavathi's thigh raised its head from the water and looked at Bavathi with what in a human would have been reproach. The serpents slowly slithered over and around the woman. Her eyes were half closed, her moist lips moving softly as if she were whispering to the snakes in adoration. Tendrils of steam wafted from the surface of the pool.

"Iskosia! Did you not hear me?"

The woman opened her eyes and stood up. Slowly she walked out of the pool, the serpents still winding around her legs, her arms, her torso, quivering and their forked tongues flickering. Bavathi stopped breathing. He always did when he saw Iskosia thus. Every single time. Those eyes that sparkled like the purest of diamonds. The smooth, wonderfully tawny skin. A waterfall of hair black as midnight at the bottom of a coal mine. Sleek legs that seemed impossibly long. Delightfully slim arms that wound about his neck as she brought her lips close to his, just barely touching. Pressing that splendid, naked body against his.

The sibilant hissing of the serpents was almost musical.

Iskosia said very gently, very softly; "If you ever again enter any room I occupy before asking my permission to do so, I will kill you. Do not think that because I favor you with the physical pleasure of my body that it makes you my equal. I am the master, you the slave. Have we an understanding?"

The hissing of the serpents stopped. It could be they were waiting for his answer as well.

"Yes. I forgot myself in my excitement. I crave thy pardon."

Iskosia removed her arms from around his neck and walked away, the serpents falling from her body and slithering back into the pool. She picked up a thick robe made from the fur of mountain wolves and wrapped it around her gorgeous body. She seated herself in a padded ivory chair, curling her legs seductively under her. "Speak. What mean you that the wenches escaped you?"

"I pursued them to the docks. There they begged the sanctuary of a sea captain. I attempted to take them but the accursed Steel Leopards arrived. Between them and the captain's men, I and my mercenaries were outnumbered. We had no choice but to flee."

"And Zenobia? She still lives? She is where?"

"On the captain's ship. His name is Sinbad."

Iskosia's response surprised Bavathi. She laughed. "The infamous Sinbad! Well, why am I not surprised? Sinbad is a friend to the Sultan of Basra. And Sinbad has long enjoyed a reputation for interfering in matters that are none of his business."

"I will cut out his heart and feed it to the jackals," Bavathi snarled. "But our immediate problem is how to kill Zenobia and her servant."

"No it is not," Iskosia replied. "How many of your men died? How many do you have left?"

"I lost six good swordsmen on the dock. Sinbad has a Viking berserker in his crew he loosed upon us. He took us completely by surprise. Between the heathen and the Steel Leopards..." Bavathi ground his teeth. "I still have the men I left here at the Abbey. Together with the men who survived that makes fifteen."

"Not enough. By now, the Steel Leopards are surely guarding Sinbad's ship. Between them and Sinbad's crew you could not even get near the

Slowly she walked out of the pool...

ship."

"Let me send word and I can have a hundred men here in a day!"

"Think you Sinbad will wait? No. He will leave with the morning tide and so must we. Prepare your men for an ocean voyage. We follow Sinbad."

"What need have we to follow the dog? You know where The Well of Apollo is, do you not?"

"I know *where* it is but not *how* to get there. I had to promise much to the demon I summoned for the location but I was unwilling to pay its price to learn the way there. I know only that Cobophia lies beyond the Sea of Jade Mist. In order to get there we need to follow Sinbad."

"How shall we know where he is going?"

In answer Iskosia looked toward the heated pool. A snake emerged from the water, leaving a glistening trail as it slid across the marble floor to its mistress. Six feet long, the golden-green serpent wriggled up the leg Iskosia outstretched for it. It wound around the leg, up the the thigh and raised up its head until it was but a few inches from Iskosia's eyes.

Although no words passed between the sorceress and the serpent, Bavathi could swear that they were communicating. The snake's forked tongue licked out and the tip of Iskosia's tongue emerged from between her ruby lips to touch the snake's. The snake unwound itself from her leg and was gone in an eye blink, sidewinding across the slick floor so quickly that to Bavathi's eyes it seemed magical. "Where does the serpent go?"

"To Sinbad's ship. It shall be our eyes there. And thus we shall know where Sinbad goes and we shall follow. But until then…" Iskosia threw back the fur to reveal her naked body and held out her arms. "…you may now properly express your regret for your earlier disrespect."

The sword belt with the huge scimitar clattered to the floor. It was joined by a trail of Bavathi's clothing as he went toward the closest thing to Paradise he had ever known in life.

❋ ❋ ❋

"Look alive there! Secure that rigging and be sure that the hold is bolted down properly! Prepare to bring the ship before the wind! Raise up tacks and stand by the braces! And sing, my brothers! Make your work light with song!" Sinbad stood at the wheel of his ship, watching as his crew made the final few preparations before setting sail. The morning wind freshened and the tide would soon be perfect for departure.

Sinbad always felt pride when he stood at the wheel of The Blue Nymph, looking at her in the way most men looked at their wives. Strong and slender she was. But delicate as well. Constructed entirely of good Ethiopian teakwood she had carried Sinbad through many a sea and storm. Sinbad's rivals spent many hours examining the ship and they offered hefty bribes for any of Sinbad's crew who would betray the secrets of the ship's construction. In truth, the modifications and retrofitting of The Blue Nymph had been designed by Sinbad and Omar and so was known only to them. The cunning Omar had the work done by many different teams of shipbuilders and artisans who only worked on specifics and never the whole. The rails and bulwarks had been masterfully carved by the finest of Persian artisans. The Blue Nymph was painted in a smoky deep blue hue but her rigging was the color of the sea itself. The bright blue square sail on the single mast billowed as if the ship itself were eager to catch it and be gone to new seas and new lands. The figurehead was of a beauteous, full-bodied mermaid whose arms seemed to be reaching for the horizon. All around her were seven starfish, representing the seven seas her captain had conquered. Her two shining eyes were crystal blue and composed of great globes of inset glass, though some swore they were two great jewels Sinbad had procured in his travels.

Omar had been down on the deck with the men as he was very much a hands-on First Mate. But now he came up on the stern. Ralf Gunarson sat there on a stout stool, sharpening his sword. Half the length of the formidable weapon on both sides were etched with runes that Ralf claimed were put there by the first of his line, the offspring of the union between a human maid and Tyr, one of his many gods. He nodded at Omar as the First Mate nodded back, then laid into his captain. "Am I not First Mate of The Blue Nymph and Master of The Crew?" he demanded wrathfully.

"Indeed you are. The best one Allah ever blew breath into!"

"Then let me do my job! The men can sing when their work is done! By Barani's Lamp, you would have them drink wine and carouse until the ship falls to pieces!"

"Fix that sour face of yours, Omar. When have we not gone on a new voyage without the crew singing as we leave port? It has become ritual for the crew of The Blue Nymph."

"They sing because they know not the foolish quest they are on."

Sinbad clapped the smaller man on the shoulder. "I did not hear any of them complain when we told them yesterday. As always, I bade them that if any man wished to remain on land he could do so and none would call him coward or shirker without answering to my sword. Did any leave?"

"No. But that is because you make light and do not tell them of the true dangers that await them. You are responsible for their lives and they have a right to know exactly what it is they are risking their lives for. How many good men have we lost in previous voyages?" Omar looked over at Ralf.

"And have you nothing to say, you deluded infidel?"

Ralf paused in his sword sharpening. "You nag like a fishwife. And still you follow Sinbad. And you would follow him into Hell gladly if he went. It is your way to pretend otherwise. But I pray to Odin that one day you will cease. It tires me to listen." The Viking resumed his sword sharpening.

"I should have known better than to ask the opinion of a heathen." Omar gestured rudely as Henri Delacrois and Tishimi Osara walked up the stairs to join them. "And here are more heroic fools to support you. I am outnumbered and out-talked. Bad enough to try and talk sense to you or Henri when the two of you are apart. But put you and the Gaul together and a sensible man has no possibility of speaking a reasonable word."

"If Sinbad would listen to aught I said we would be heading for the fleshpots of Selon. It is said that diamonds flow in its rivers and pearls are in its valleys." Henri flashed a grin that was an easy rival to his captain's for sheer wickedness.

Omar snorted in disgust. "Truly it is written; trust in Allah…"

Sinbad, Ralf, Tishimi and Henri all finished that most favorite of sayings aboard The Blue Nymph which they had all heard too many times to count in their travels together: "…but tie up your camel."

Haroun called up the stern, "Ready to weigh anchor, captain!"

"Then do so and let us be off!"

Unseen by all, the long, sinuous body of a golden green snake swam towards the anchor chain of The Blue Nymph. Silently, it slid up the chain, even as the crew hauled it up. The snake went up and up, slithering through the chain's opening. So quickly was the snake moving that none saw it, even young Haroun who was known to have the sharpest eyes among the crew. He saw something out of the corner of his eye and his head snapped around so quickly that he felt a twinge of pain in his neck. But he saw nothing. He shrugged and bent back to his work, supposing that it must have been a rat for every ship had its share of the vermin. He chose to look upon it as a sign from Allah that their voyage was not doomed. Sailors well knew that rats on board a ship was not something to worry about. It was when you didn't see any…ah, there was a true cause for worry.

The Blue Nymph's sail filled with the strong wind and she majestically sailed out of the port of Basra. Sinbad steered his ship toward the open sea. He looked around him. At his four stalwart friends at his side. At the valiant crew who sang as they worked. He felt The Blue Nymph respond to his handling of the wheel as if it were a living being. Never did he feel more alive than when he embarked on a new voyage. Yes, this was his true destiny, the life he wished to live and he needed or wanted no other to be truly happy. Among all the men in the world, was there any more blessed or favored than he?

Unseen by Sinbad or his friends, a pair of hidden reptilian eyes looked at him with human hate.

Zenobia hobbled up on deck, using her staff and the lovely Farah to assist her as she laboriously walked up the steps to join Sinbad and the others. "Good morning to you, captain."

"And a good morning to you as well, old mother. A fine day for a voyage, is it not?"

"Any day I wake up and greet the dawn is a good day," Zenobia cackled, showing a mouth surprisingly full of teeth for one so aged.

"And do you find the accommodations of The Blue Nymph to your satisfaction, Mistress Farah?" Sinbad asked.

"Indeed I do, captain. And your friend Tishimi is most courteous and gracious to our needs."

"I am well pleased, then. So, now to business! Wither shall we go, old mother?"

"The Sea of Jade Mist, captain. How long will it take us to get there?"

"Depends. We have never been there so I have no idea how long it would take."

"What? I thought you have been everywhere, Captain Sinbad!"

"Not the Sea of Jade Mist," Omar grumbled. "Never had we the need or desire to go there."

"Omar, how long would you say it would take us?"

Omar looked up at the sky as he did his calculations. "We can have the men row if the wind dies down to keep up our speed. Our chances of running into pirates is not great as we sail in a direction sane men do not go. And though they be murderous, motherless scum, the pirates who sail these waters are not mad. If we do not run into any storms and we shouldn't this time of year, my best estimate is five to seven days."

"There you have it. Make yourselves comfortable, ladies. We have at least five days to get to know each other better." Sinbad smiled at Farah. She blushed slightly and dropped her eyes. Sinbad gestured to Omar to take over at the wheel.

The serpent slithered away to find a place to sleep away the day. It would do its searching at night when all would be asleep except for the watch.

Back at the port of Basra, when Sinbad's ship was but a dot on the horizon, another ship put out. The Honorable Wolf was larger, wider.

Nowhere near as fast or as trim as The Blue Nymph. But then again, few ships were. Bavathi the Executioner and Iskosia stood by the wheel with Captain Zibo. His prematurely white hair fluttered like a flag in the strong wind. He shouted orders to his crew but the orders given to him by Iskosia were spoken in a soft murmur barely above a whisper. "Remember to stay well back, Captain Zibo. Above all, we do not wish to alert Sinbad that we follow him."

"I understand. And fear not. I have had some experience in this. I know how to follow a ship. We run with no lights at night so that we can draw closer and keep their lights in sight. At dawn, we will pull back."

"Excellent. Serve me well in this and besides what I have already paid you will be further rewarded."

Captain Zibo nodded. Bavathi and Iskosia drew away from him so that they could speak in private without being overheard. "You have given instructions to your men?"

Bavathi nodded. "They will keep themselves at the ready for my signal when I give the word."

"Excellent. I did not inform Captain Zibo of our ultimate destination. It could be when he learns where we are going he may balk. If that happens, we must be ready to take the ship."

"These sea scum are no match for my trained fighters. Cut down a few and the rest will fall in line."

Iskosia nodded. "When night falls I will see what transpires on board Sinbad's ship through the eyes of my snake."

The crew of The Blue Nymph went to bed early at Omar's insistence. It was one of his rules that Sinbad did not interfere with. Omar did not put up with any foolishness when on a voyage and he demanded that the crew be well rested. After the evening meal, the men were allowed two hours for their personal amusement as well as a dram of wine. Then it was lights out and to bed. Tishimi usually took to bed herself as she herself preferred to retire early and rise early. In fact, Tishimi liked to arise before dawn and practice her katas on deck before the crew woke up and began the day's work. Ralf also went to bed early. Since there was no carousing, wenching or serious drinking to be done on the ship, he saw no reason to stay up. Omar also went to bed early as he believed in leading by example.

But for Sinbad El Ari and Henri Delacrois it was another matter. They liked to stay up well past midnight, telling each other stories, drinking wine, singing songs or boasting of their romantic conquests. They were boon companions, these two. Well suited in temperament and nature. And although Henri presented the image of laziness and disinterest in anything save women, games of chance and sleeping, his friends knew otherwise. At best a fair swordsman but put a bow in his hands with a quiver of arrows on his back and there wasn't a deadlier man to be found. And when it came to woodcraft and tracking it was said that Henri Delacrois could track a black ant on the ebony sands of The Black Desert at midnight.

Sinbad asked Henri to accompany him to the cabin where the wounded man lay recuperating. Two of the Steel Leopards were on guard outside the cabin at all times. Sinbad gestured for one of them to unlock the door. He stepped inside while Henri stood leaning on the doorway.

The wounded man lay on the bunk on his side facing away from the door. He did not budge.

The attention of Sinbad, Henri and the two Steel Leopards were on the man lying on the bunk. That is why no one saw the golden-green snake slither silently inside the cabin. It slid along the wall, until coming to a rat hole. The snake slipped inside. It turned around so that it could see out.

Sinbad spoke in a voice that contained none of his usual boyish gusto. This voice was as serious as a dagger held to an unprotected throat. "Sit up."

The man turned around, he looked Sinbad up and down. "And who are you?"

It was Henri who answered. "Watch the tone of your voice, fellow. You speak to Captain Sinbad of The Blue Nymph. Do so with a humble tongue."

The man sat up on the bunk. "I suppose that courtesy demands I thank you for tending to my wounds."

"What is your name?"

"Redor of Osden."

"Osden?" Henri said. "You are a long way from home. Osden is past Old Lorosine and that is so far off it makes my head ache to think of how long it takes to get there."

Sinbad returned to business. "If you truly feel that you are in my debt then you can tell me what Bavathi and the sorceress he serves have planned?"

Redor grunted, scratching his thick beard. "While I appreciate you saving my life that does not mean it belongs to you. I gave my oath of allegiance to Bavathi and it is he I call master."

One of the Steel Leopards growled, "Leave him to us, Captain Sinbad. We'll make the cur talk."

"No. I respect a man who keeps his word. Even if he gave that word to a coward who makes war on women. And I allow no brutality or torture on my ship." Sinbad said firmly. He turned back to Redor. "You will be kept in this cabin under lock and key. Make no trouble and you'll be treated fairly. You have my word on that. You also have my word that the first complaint I hear from any concerning you and I myself will pitch you over the side."

Redor rubbed his side. "You have my promise I will make no trouble, captain. I would not like to see that blond madman of yours again."

Sinbad had to chuckle at that. He and Henri left the cabin which was at once securely locked. Sinbad said to them, "I see no need for two of you to be on guard all the time. I think the fellow means what he says. He won't be a problem. From now on, one guard will suffice."

The men bowed slightly. "Thank you, Captain Sinbad."

"And what about you, Henri? What say we retire to my cabin? I have a cask of very fine Cerissian wine I have not yet sampled."

"You need not ask twice, my friend. Let us go. And you can finish telling me that tale about the Spanish goatherd's daughter..."

Inside the cabin, Redor once again stretched out on the bunk to return to sleep. So he did not see the snake emerge from the rat hole and slowly, silently move across the floor toward him. Driven by the human intelligence of Iskosia who looked through its eyes, the snake drew closer.

In her cabin aboard The Honorable Wolf, Iskosia lay on her bunk, her naked body trembling, the muscles of her limbs rippling. She had locked her door and two of Bavathi's men stood without as she gave strict word that she was not to be disturbed by anyone for any reason whatsoever. She was in full communion with the snake and her concentration could not be broken. The danger to her if that happened was great.

Through the snake's eyes she saw Sinbad talking with Redor and at once she saw her chance to kill Zenobia, Sinbad and as many of the crew as possible. Once Sinbad was dead, his crew would be demoralized and no threat at all. And with Zenobia dead she would have no threat to her power. She would bathe in the cosmic waters of The Well of Apollo and return to Basra a goddess. And then the world would tremble!

The snake inched upwards, the length of its six foot long body raising up in the air. It crawled on the bunk, sliding across Redor's body. The man grunted, half turned and gasped in horror at seeing a snake's head an inch from his own. The snake took advantage of the gasp and dived into Redor's open mouth.

Redor tried to scream but could not as his throat was filled with snake. The creature thrust its way down his throat, forcing its way deeper and deeper down into Redor's body. In utter terror, Redor laid hold of the thing, tried to yank it out of his mouth, his throat. By all the gods he could feel it in his stomach!

Redor fell off the bunk with a thud, rolling over and over still trying to pull the loathsome creature out of him. He banged up against a wall, blood spurting from his nostrils, his eyes bulging out of the sockets as if they would burst. He tried to scream but panting squeals were the best he could do.

With one hand he held onto the wall, staggering to his feet. The other hand still held onto the snake. Or what was left of it as most of the vile serpent was now in his body. Redor stumbled over to the door, pounded on it with his free hand.

"Quiet in there!"

Redor tried again to scream but a only a pitiful gargle emerged from him. It was all he could manage with a throat full of snake. He banged again. He kicked.

"I said quiet, blast your hide! Did you not hear Captain Sinbad say that he would cast you over the side if you made trouble?"

Redor fell over backwards. His arms and legs thrashed wildly about. His abdomen heaved and bulged as if the snake were performing obscene acrobatics within.

One Steel Leopard said to the other, "Sinbad didn't say that we couldn't give the cur a rap on the head if he became rambunctious. And it may loosen his tongue at last."

"Aye. Here, give over the key and I'll unlock the door. We'll see if we cannot provide a cure for whatever ails the fellow."

Redor rolled over on his stomach, vomited up blood and chunks of his intestines. His eyes rolled madly in their sockets. The door opened and the Steel Leopards stopped, their own eyes opening wider. "Poison!" one shouted. "He's been poisoned!"

"Don't speak such foolishness! What reason would…" The Steel Leopard never finished his thought. Redor spun around with frightening speed. He raised up his arms. They vibrated like the wings of a hummingbird. And then, with a hideous splitting, ripping sound, his arms tore open as snake heads emerged from the shattered limbs. The human flesh fell away to show that now Redor had huge golden-green snakes for arms!

The snake heads whipped out to wrap around the bodies of The Steel

Redor...tried to yank it out.

Leopards. They never had a chance to draw their swords at all. Redor slammed them against each other, their armor clanging like a bell of warning.

The crew of The Blue Nymph piled out of their bunks and hammocks, shouting excited questions back and forth, turning out on deck, thinking that the night watch was rousing the alarm.

Sinbad emerged from his cabin, tankard in hand. "Omar! What is all that infernal noise?"

Omar dashed past Sinbad, winding his sash about his waist. "I'm going up on deck now, Captain!"

The cabin being used as Redor's cell was at the other end of the ship from Sinbad's cabin, the crew quarters and the cabin shared by Henri, Ralf and Omar. Tishimi had her own small cabin and she emerged from this, her scabbarded katana in her hand. "Are we being attacked?"

"Damned if I know. Tishimi, you stay with the old woman and Farah. Henri, come with me."

Redor's snake arms withdrew from their grisly work. The quivering pieces of meat on the bloody floor could not be said to resemble anything human. Redor fell on the floor, rolling around and around in the hideous mess, moaning and hissing as his legs twisted and writhed.

In her cabin on The Honorable Wolf, Iskosia's arms described patterns in the air above her. Her eyes had gone completely red and her skin shone with a thick coating of sweat. She muttered words in a language that had been dead and forgotten before bright Atlantis sunk beneath the waves. It was the language used by those who worshipped Satha, the Father of All Serpents. Over the ages Satha had become deified and worshipped under other names such as Ophion, Set, Jormungandr, Wallungqua and Naga. But Satha was his true name. And the language of Satha was understood by all his serpentine children. And humans who understood and spoke that language could command the scaly folk. Couple that with the hideous magical powers commanded by Iskosia.

Sinbad and most of his crew were on deck. Some of the men were busy searching below. The remaining three Steel Leopards looked around for their fellows. "Have any of you seen aught of Banarill and Warcha?" one called out.

Sinbad himself answered. "The last I saw of them they were guarding the prisoner."

The aft access hatch burst upwards in a shower of splintered wood. And writhing from the innards of The Blue Nymph emerged terror.

Redor's legs had fused together into a single, thick snake's tail. His torso was still human, for whatever that was worth. His snake arms lashed about wildly, the forked tongues flicking out. Redor's mouth was now full of hundreds of needle sharp fangs that overlapped. A banshee scream of insane rage burst from his throat as he lunged directly at Sinbad.

Sinbad leaped backwards with blinding speed, his scimitar whipping out to block the thrusts of both snake heads. The keen blade slashed at the tough skin of the snake arms, scoring deep hits but not drawing any blood. The crew whooped and hollered as they leaped forward to defend their captain, Redor swung his arms like living whips and battered the crewmen aside as if they were children. Redor slithered in pursuit of Sinbad who snatched up the lid of a water barrel and used it as a shield, fending off one striking head while engaging the other with his scimitar, keeping those fearsome fangs away.

From his vantage point in the stern, Henri let loose with an arrow. Before that shaft barely cleared the bow, he was nocking another arrow. As soon as that one was away, a third was being nocked even as the first one hit home, taking Redor in the back. Howling in anger more than pain, Redor twisting around to catch the next two arrows in the chest. They had no effect on the snake man and he undulated with horribly frightening speed at the archer, one snake arm going out, fangs dripping.

From out of nowhere, Ralf shoved the Gaul aside and slammed his axe full into the side of the snake's head. Green blood gouted from the terrible gash the axe inflicted. A normal creature would have been decapitated by such a mighty stroke. But this being a creature of sorcery, it had supernatural stamina and resistance to mortal weapons. Still, the sight of blood was a welcome one.

"It's flesh and blood, my brothers!" Sinbad shouted triumphantly. "And if it's flesh and blood then it can die!" He leaped to the attack, slashing at Redor's back with his scimitar. Omar shouted orders at the crew. While Sinbad and Ralf kept Redor occupied, crewmen laid hands on ropes and fashioned lassos out of them. Upon Omar's direction, they tossed one noose over one snake arm and pulled it tight. Redor's head turned to glare balefully at them, snapping and hissing hate. The other snake arm was similarly lassoed and that arm pulled tight.

"Down! DOWN!" Omar bellowed. "Get it DOWN so that we may cut off its cursed head!"

The plan was an excellent one but Redor was not co-operating. His arms may have been trapped but not so his tail. It lashed up, around and out like a giant living whip of flesh, sending Sinbad, Omar and the crew holding his snake arms flying.

Ralf leaped from the stern, bellowing his war cry. He wrapped a thick arm around Redor's neck and lifted the axe, intending to crush the snake man's head. One of Redor's arms reached up and around and seized hold of the Viking by the waist. The fangs couldn't pierce through the thick leather vest Ralf wore but he was still plucked off Redor's back. Ralf slashed out futilely with his axe, snarling; "Foul! Oh, foul!" With an ease that bordered on contemptuous, Redor flung the Viking up and away. Ralf disappeared into the darkness .

Sinbad came in with a mighty double-handed strike that this time drew blood as the scimitar bit deeply into the torso. Redor screeched like a stepped on dog. He was all wildly flailing limbs and tail that smashed into the decks, the railings. Insanely, the snake man rolled around and around, the snake heads snapping and gnashing at everything within reach. Sinbad fought to get in closer as he felt that if could just get in one good clean strike at the unprotected throat or heart.

"Stand aside, Captain Sinbad!" the voice coming from Zenobia was not that of an old woman. She had the voice of a warrior now as she stepped forward, thrusting her staff up into Redor's face. A burst of blue white electricity arced from the staff's head to bridge the gap between and struck Redor full in the face. The snake man lurched backwards, the snake heads hissing and snarling.

Sinbad ran at full speed, leaped up and struck out with both booted feet into Redor's chest. The snake man slammed up against the railing as Tishimi came in with her katana. Washed in the blood of her father, the blade itself was a powerful weapon against magic and proved so as it sliced cleanly through Redor's left arm. The stump of the arm gushed stinking green blood while the severed head flopped around on deck, hissing and snapping.

Omar directed several crew men with long poles to charge Redor and they did so with all their might, the poles smashing into Redor's chest. The snake man went over the railing and fell into the water, screaming and thrashing. He hit the water with a tremendous splash and The Blue Nymph continued on, leaving the damned creature behind but they could still hear its screaming and wailing.

Omar wiped away the sweat from his forehead. " Sinbad, what was that thing?"

"It was the prisoner. Somehow he transformed into that hell spawn!"

"It was Iskosia." Zenobia said as she hobbled forward. Her voice was still strong but it was obvious that working her magic wearied the old woman. She leaned heavily on her staff. Farah hurried to help her. Zenobia smiled her thanks and resumed her explanation. "Through her magic she did this. Undoubtedly she sent a snake aboard your ship before we left port, Captain Sinbad. Using her foul arts she fused man and serpent together in that horrid creature."

"By the blood of my ancestors," Sinbad whispered. "Then there is no telling what she may know of our plans."

Zenobia nodded. "I am afraid that is true."

Sinbad kicked at the severed snake head. "Omar, get this deck cleaned up. See to the wounded. Send some men below to check for damage. And…" Sinbad's orders were interrupted by a familiar bellow from high up above. Everybody looked up to see Ralf Gunarson clinging precariously to the very top of the mast which he had grabbed when he was thrown upwards.

"For the love of Odin get me down from here!"

Dawn arrived with the crew of The Blue Nymph greeting it with relief. No one even thought of going back to sleep after the attack so the work day started early. Ralf was assisted down from the top of the mast. The snake head thrown over the side. The bloody deck washed down. The dead and injured seen to. Five dead bodies lay on the freshly washed deck. Three Steel Leopards and two of The Blue Nymph's crew had been killed by the snake man. Three more crewmen would not be able to work due to broken bones suffered in the attack.

Omar reported to the stern where Sinbad stood at the wheel, sailing his ship over the placid waters. His eyes were fixed on the far horizon. Omar cleared his throat reproachfully before starting in. "I've got five less men now to work this ship, Sinbad."

"Enough, Omar. Any other time our game of banter amuses me but not now. This is serious."

"By the beard of Allah, think you not that I am not being serious as well? I like not how this voyage is going, Sinbad. We have not yet reached our destination and already we look at five dead men and three who will not be able to work ship for months. We will have to support them and their families as well."

"As we always have done, Omar. I take care of my men." Sinbad placed a firm hand on his friend's shoulder. "We have been through worse."

Omar sighed in resignation. "It is in the hands of Allah. It shall be as He wills." Omar went back to his work, passing Farah on her way up. Sinbad motioned for a crewman to take over. "Maintain course."

"Aye, captain."

Sinbad took Farah's arm and they stepped further to the rear of the stern so that they could speak in private. "How is Zenobia?"

"She is sleeping. At her age any amount of expenditure to exercise her mystic talents tires her. And she will need her strength to direct us to Cobophia."

"Exactly how old is Zenobia?"

Farah shook her head. "I know not. She was old when I was a young girl, left by my mother at the abbey. My mother did not want me. She delighted in dancing, carousing and pleasuring men. That was the life she wanted."

"Praise be to Allah she had the wisdom to place you in the care of those who would provide you with a decent home and a decent life."

Farah smiled. "I have heard the stories, Captain Sinbad. You have no trouble with enjoying the company of women of that sort."

"Those are fully grown women who have made their choice and who live with it. There is a difference between that and young girls who are never given that choice and are forced into such a life against their will." Sinbad placed a gentle finger under her chin and lifted her head. "And what of your choices? By Barani's Lamp, girl...you are beautiful enough to win the eye of any number of sultans or caliphs!"

"And be but another pampered pet in a seraglio with other women all willing to scratch out each other's eyes for the slightest chance of winning favor from a fat sultan or caliph more interested in his horses or his treasure than in a wife?" Farah replied, her voice filling with a heat that she had not yet shown until now. "No thank you! There are many forms of slavery, Sinbad and that is not one to my liking!"

Sinbad let his hand fall away and bowed his head slightly. "My apologies, Mistress Farah. Oftentimes I speak my mind without thought. I did not mean to give offense."

Farah reached out a hand to take his. "Your apologies are not necessary. You are known as a good man, Sinbad. Zenobia told me that you are the only man she would trust to see that she gets to The Well of Apollo."

"And why is it so important that we get to The Well of Apollo before this Iskosia? What mischief does she intend?"

"The only mortal who may bathe in the cosmic waters of The Well of Apollo is she who has been sanctified by The Mother of The Phoenix. And that is not Iskosia. If she dares to bathe in the cosmic waters unsanctified there is no telling what chaos may be unleashed upon the Earth."

"And who is sanctified? You?" Sinbad stepped closer.

"I? No. I am far too young to be accorded such an honor. Why do you ask?"

Sinbad stepped even closer. "Oh, it just seems that there is always some such silly condition for a woman who gives herself over to a religious order. Such as she cannot be kissed."

Farah looked up into Sinbad's mischievous blue eyes and said softly; "Rest assured, Captain Sinbad that I can indeed be kissed. And more."

❀ ❀ ❀

Bavathi The Executioner escorted the cook to Iskosia's cabin. Bavathi himself always watched as her meals were prepared, one hand on his scimitar. Ever since she had taken to her cabin and not come out, there had been grumblings from the crew:

"Any fool can see that she is a witch! She will bring the curse of Allah down upon us!"

"A woman has no place on a ship. I care not how much gold she has!"

"What madness is it to sail with no course and no chart to tell us the way?"

But the grumblings ceased when Bavathi or his men were near. Still, he was taking no chances that Iskosia's meals might be poisoned.

Once they reached her cabin, Bavathi sent the cook away. Which he did so quite gladly. Bavathi knocked on the door. "'Tis I, beloved."

The door opened and the wooden tray exchanged hands. Bavathi shuddered as he looked at Iskosia's hands. Once smooth and tan they were now scaly, taloned horrors. She set the tray down and whispered through the narrow crack a fingernail wide which was all the width she dared open the door, "What is the news?"

"The crew still grumbles and even the captain is now saying that if the crew could see you on deck for even a brief moment it would dispel the rumors that you work evil magic down here."

"That is impossible! I need another day, two at most to regain my natural appearance."

"Take all the time you require. I can keep this ship in line. But I still do not understand."

"Magic has its price, whether it be worked for good or for ill. My consciousness was linked to that of the snake's and thence to the human agent it worked through. Once it was injured, it forced my consciousness back into my body but I brought some of the snake's spiritual essence with me and it reshaped my body. I can regain my normal form but I must have time! Time you must buy for me!"

"I shall. But what of Sinbad's ship? How shall we follow it now?"

"I have one trick up my sleeve but we must wait until we reach the Sea of Jade Mist. When we have done so, come to me." The door closed silently and Bavathi went back up on deck. Captain Zibo, upon spying him, walked over to ask, "Is the Lady Iskosia well?"

"Well enough. Why do you ask?"

"The men continue to grumble."

"Can you not control your own crew, man? What manner of captain are you?"

Zibo spread his hands in frustration. "Your gold is good enough for me. For what you have paid me I know enough to keep my mouth shut. But sailors are superstitious. And they love to make up stories."

"Who would you say is the one with the biggest mouth?"

Without hesitation, Zibo gestured at a sullen-eyed, thickly muscled sailor who stood near the railing with several others. He openly looked back at Bavathi with hostility. "That is Essr. He complains constantly about everything. He is the sort that always looks for a problem where there is none."

"Is he a good worker?"

"Not that good."

Bavathi nodded and strode directly for Essr, unsheathing that fearful scimitar. Essr's shipmates scattered like startled chickens. Essr brought up his hands, shouting, "A moment to speak, master! I beg of you, just a moment!"

"You have talked too much already." The sword hummed through the air and Essr's head tumbled to the deck. So quickly did it happen that the mouth still worked, trying to form words and the eyes rolled madly.

Bavathi picked up the body with one hand and heaved it over the side. It hit the water with a tremendous splash and was gone. Bavathi picked up the head, walked with it over to the mast. He slammed his dagger into the wood and tied the head by its long hair to the dagger. Bavathi glared at the sailors who had watched this grisly display.

"The next man who grumbles, complains or says a word against my lady will have his head join this one. If there be any who has an issue with this, step forward now that we may resolve it."

It occurred to the crew that they had best see to their work and they did so with a dedication and enthusiasm that would have brought tears of joy

Magic has its price…

to flow from the eyes of Omar would that he had been there to see sailors working as he believed they should work.

Bavathi strode over to Captain Zibo, who bowed low. "My thanks, O Executioner. You have rid me of a troublesome flea in my ear."

"It is the last time, thou liverless cur!"

"I beg thy pardon, master? What have I done to offend thee?"

"You do not keep your men in their proper place is thy offense! I am not here to do your work! You call thyself captain?"

"I do."

"Then conduct yourself as such! Else find your head on your own mast!"

The next four days aboard The Blue Nymph passed without incident. The bodies of the men that had been killed were buried at sea. They were wrapped in sailcloth and weights were tied on their feet. Prayers were said and that was that. Death itself was a crewmate on every ship that sailed the seas. It came fast and it came when it wished. There was no use in bemoaning and wailing. This was the life they had chosen.

Repairs were made while they sailed and Omar was much pleased. Anything that kept the minds of the crew off their destination was a good thing. Tishimi spent time with Zenobia, talking with the old woman about art, mysticism and philosophy. Much as Tishimi enjoyed talking with her male companions, she found they were…lacking in certain areas she liked to discuss. Ralf sharpened his weapons. Henri spent most of his time gambling with such members of the crew who were foolish enough to do so.

And Sinbad spent much time in his cabin. When asked he insisted he was reading up on Cobophia as he had a book written by a long dead explorer from Myrthia who had set down his exploits in that legendary land. It was noticed by Sinbad's friends that Farah also seemed to be difficult to find on those occasions when Sinbad sequestered himself in his cabin. Doubtless it was a coincidence.

And on the fifth day the ship stirred at the cry of sharp-eyed Haroun up in the crow's nest; "Behold! We have arrived, my brothers! There be The Sea of Jade Mist dead ahead!"

Those crew members not on deck heard the yelling and stomping of feet as their fellows on duty dropped whatever they were doing and rushed to look. They came up from below to join their cries of astonishment with their mates.

Sinbad emerged from his cabin, winding his sash about his waist. Nimbly he bounded up the stairs to the wheel where Omar stood, already bringing The Blue Nymph about. "Do you see it, Sinbad?" Omar said wonderingly.

"Aye, good friend. I do!"

A shimmering hazy curtain of gentle green mist in front of the ship stretched for as far as they could see to the port and to the starboard. Ahead of them was naught but green. Sinbad heard the excited voices of the crew:

"It is said that one could sail for a year and a day and still not sail around the Jade Mist! One must go through it get anywhere!"

"But who can find their way once within? None can see neither sun nor stars!"

"It is the work of demons and devils! Sinbad should turn the ship around and return to Basra!"

"Bah! We have come this far! And what is there to fear inside of mere fog?"

"Better to ask that question of our shipmates Riles and Tuliso who we buried mere days ago."

"Pfui! Truly it is written that a fool has his own answer on the tip of his tongue!"

"Where is Zenobia?" Sinbad asked.

"I am here, captain." The old woman emerged on deck, being helped by Farah. "My apologies for not arriving sooner. It took me some time to find Farah so that she may assist me on deck." Zenobia's voice may have been stern but her eyes twinkled with merriment. "I see we have arrived at our destination."

"Not quite, old mother. We have arrived at The Sea of Jade Mist. That is still quite a ways away from our destination of Cobophia." Sinbad nimbly ran down the stairs to join Zenobia and Farah. "But you said that you could direct us straight there. I must confess that I am curious to see how you do it."

"But you are the great Captain Sinbad! Could you not take us there?"

Sinbad chuckled as he enjoyed being teased as much as he enjoyed teasing others. "Ah, but even as great a sea captain as I must have charts and stars, revered one. Now, if you prefer I can steer by guess and by Allah but there is no telling when we would arrive at Cobophia. If ever we did and not sail right past it in the mist!"

Zenobia joined him in a good laugh and then said, "Well, we cannot have that, now can we? If you will be so good as to take the wheel of your ship, captain and wait for my signal."

"And what signal will that be?"

"You will know it. And when you do, be swift and follow! Understand?"

"I do. Everyone to their stations! Tishimi, stay with Farah and Zenobia! Haroun!"

From high up, Haroun yelled down; "Aye, my captain?"

"Come down, refresh yourself and sleep for two hours! Then I want you back up in the nest! Daveng, you take his place! Omar, with me!"

Farah helped Zenobia up the prow of the ship. Once she got there, the old woman seemed to gain a surge of strength from some deep reserve and waved Farah back. Zenobia held the staff vertically in both of her wrinkled hands. Her mouth worked as she spoke under her breath. No mere mumblings did she utter. No, she spoke words that were older than the oldest kingdoms of the Earth. They were words in a language spoken by gods and demons in the very beginning of the world. It was a language few mortals could speak because the words themselves held such power that a mere mortal brain could not remember them. Zenobia's voice grew louder and stronger as she continued her spell making. The staff in her hands began to glow as if a fire were starting from inside. The crew drew back, well away from the frail old woman who suddenly did not seem so frail or so old.

Ralf Gunarson muttered prayers to Odin and Tyr as he joined Sinbad, Tishimi, Omar and Henri. "Are you sure she knows what she is doing?" Ralf asked of everyone and no one.

It was Henri who took it upon himself to answer; "it would appear it is too late for us to be asking such questions, no?"

"By The Beard of Allah," Omar gasped, "Look you there!"

The head of Zenobia's staff burst into a beacon that lanced forward like a living bolt of resplendent, purest starlight. It cut through the emerald fog like a white hot poker through ice. Zenobia herself was haloed in a sparkling fluorescent curtain whirling around her. And words still poured from her mouth.

"By the blood of my ancestors," Sinbad shouted. "This is the signal! We must follow the light through the mist and it will take us straight to The Land of The Frozen Sun! We go! Hurry!"

Omar went to work, dashing down to the deck and shouting orders while Sinbad turned the huge wheel. The gigantic sail majestically caught the wind and The Blue Nymph surged forward, agile as a porpoise as she bounded over the water toward The Sea of Jade Mist. The brilliant beam of intense white light went before the ship, into the emerald fog. And then, The Blue Nymph entered.

Immediately the mist engulfed them. It was like no fog any of them had ever been before. It actually smelled quite pleasing as if imbued with some mystic scent that tickled the nose. But it was thick enough that once they were inside, they could not see more than twenty feet or so in front of them or to the sides. Past that, all was green. Even though the light from the sun reached them, it was impossible for any on the ship to catch sight of that orb.

Zenobia lifted her staff in both hands high above her head and brought it down upon the deck. The end of the staff stuck into the strong wood without piercing it. The curtain of light swirled away into nothingness as Zenobia fell back into the waiting arms of Farah.

Sinbad left the wheel and Omar immediately took over. Followed by Ralf, Henri and Tishimi he ran over to where Zenobia lay on the deck, her head in Farah's lap. Sinbad knelt next to her, taking both of her hands in his. She looked so feeble and so weak that Sinbad shouted for the ship's doctor. Zenobia cackled weakly. "Do not fret thyself, Sinbad. I will not leave this life just yet." She drew in a deep breath. "It costs much for me these days to work my magic. Each effort leaves me sorely drained and it takes longer and longer to regain my strength." She pointed at the staff and the brilliant beam of light. "Let none touch my staff lest the magic is spoiled. Follow the light. It will take us directly to Cobophia. But have a care once we clear the mist! You must beware." Zenobia plainly had more to say but exhaustion overcame her at last and she simply lapsed into unconsciousness.

"She will be fine, I assure you," Farah said. "She needs sleep now more than anything else."

"Ralf, take her to her cabin."

"Aye." The bearded young giant bent and lifted Zenobia in those massively muscled arms as gently as if she were but a newborn babe and followed Farah.

"She was telling you to beware once we clear the mist," Tishimi said. "Which means there is some peril awaiting us once we do so."

Sinbad stroked his beard, looking at the beam of light. "Aye."

"And how long do we sail through this infernal fog?" Henri wanted to know.

"As long as it takes, my friend. As long as it takes."

The star bright beam of light unwavering pointed straight ahead and so The Blue Nymph went further and further into The Sea of Jade Mist. How long they were in there, not a member of the crew could tell. Once inside the emerald fog, they could not tell how much time had passed since they could not see the sun. They would sleep, wake up and still it was daylight.

"Surely we must be near Cobophia," Henri Delacrois said. He had just come up on deck and walked up to the stern, yawning and scratching his sides. "I have slept thrice and still it is daylight."

"I have slept twice," Omar said.

"As have I," Tishimi said. "How can this be?"

"We have crossed into another realm," Ralf said in that booming voice like the rumbling wheels of a war chariot. "No man may say how long anything lasts when they cannot agree on how long it takes."

Sinbad did not join in the conversation. He stood resolutely at the wheel of his ship, his eyes fixed on the beam of light. He had taken all his meals at the wheel and slept curled up on a chair he had brought from his quarters. The legs of the chair fitted into special slots so that it could be bolted down firmly and not slide across the deck.

The air had lost the rich fragrance it had held when they had first sailed into the mist. Or perhaps they had simply grown used to it. Since there was no way of telling how long they had been sailing in The Sea of Jade Mist, what man could say?

His friends did not say anything to Sinbad to disturb his concentration. They had seen him like this before. All his senses were so finely tuned to his ship and to the motion of the ocean that it was as if Sinbad could actually feel his way through where no ordinary sailor could. Both Omar and Sinbad had learned their trade by way of their training with the renowned Sindhi Sailors and even among them Sinbad had distinguished himself with his uncanny instincts.

Now he spoke; "Omar."

"Aye, Sinbad?"

"Take a sounding."

"Aye. Leadsman! Take a sounding!"

The leadsman jumped to his work. He cast the sounding line over the starboard side and they heard the splash of the lead plummet. A few heartbeats later, the leadsman sang out "Full fathom seven!"

Sinbad nodded to himself. He called up to Haroun back up in the crow's nest. "Keep a sharp eye up there!"

"Aye, Captain!"

Everyone aboard ship was quiet. It was as if they all were straining to hear something. But all that could be heard was the slap of water against the sides of The Blue Nymph, the creaking of the rigging, the sail snapping in the strong wind that moved the ship but not the emerald fog.

And then, Sinbad's voice rang out with total command; "All hands look alive!"

Ten seconds later, Haroun bawled, "Captain Sinbad! Captain Sinbad! Rocks dead ahead! ROCKS DEAD AHEAD!"

The Blue Nymph burst from The Sea of Jade Mist into clear air. The sun shone brightly in the sky at high noon. The waters around the ship were now turbulent and The Blue Nymph heaved to port as it was caught up in the swell of the furious waves.

"By Odin's Beard!" Ralf exclaimed, desperately hanging onto the rigging. "Those be not mere rocks, my friends!"

The Viking warrior spoke rightly. What emerged from the turbulent waters were massive, giant stone heads, hands and arms. Some of the heads were completely out of the water, some barely sticking out, with only the eyes showing. Some of the hands were pointing, or holding globes or scrolls.

Sinbad's sinewy hands manipulated the wheel, playing it as skillfully and as lightly as a master musician playing a lyre. Turning the ship to port, barely avoiding a gigantic arm holding aloft a torch. It was a maze of sunken statues that The Blue Nymph had to navigate and even in such dire straits Sinbad wondered what sort of cataclysm could have occurred to have sunk so many gigantic statues.

Up in the crow's nest, Haroun frantically hung on. The sailors on deck slid helplessly this way and that, trying to grab onto something, anything as The Blue Nymph got caught in a wave and twirled about as if it were nothing but a cork.

Sinbad whipped the wheel back the other way, turning The Blue Nymph to starboard. A wave heaved underneath the ship, forcing it toward port, right toward a giant head that seemed to mock Sinbad with sightless marble eyes. Sinbad turned the ship into the swell of the wave, seeking to use it to skirt around the massive head lest they be smashed directly into it. "Hang on!" Sinbad sang out. Water sheeted over the stern, drenching Sinbad. He laughed as if he had not a care or worry. He might as well have been in a tavern and not at the wheel of his beloved ship, fighting to keep it from being smashed and his crew killed.

The Blue Nymph listed to one side as the swelling wave pushed it at the giant head. Sinbad heaved on the wheel, the muscles in his arms and shoulders standing out like woven cords under the dark skin. And The Blue Nymph responded to the demand from her master, leaping as if it were alive, coming so close to the giant head that the paint on that side of the ship was scraped off from stem to stern. And then the ship passed the head and continued on, leaving behind the maze of half-sunken statues.

Sinbad's friends shakily got to their feet as his merry laughter filled the air. "What do you down there, my friends? You missed a truly remarkable feat of seamanship!"

"You must forgive me, Sinbad," Henri replied sourly. "I have this aversion to watching my own death."

"And yet you look remarkably alive to me. Did you not think I would bring you through calamity with a whole skin?"

"You looked just as worried as the rest of us when we emerged from the green fog and saw those statues," Tishimi said.

"Must have been the water in your eyes that blurred your vision," Sinbad replied airily.

"Doubtless."

"Look!" Haroun bellowed. "Cobophia! It must be!"

Ahead of them they could all see the Land of The Frozen Sun. A broad expanse of beach with blinding white sand. And beyond that, a forest of almost supernaturally deep green. The staff's light changed angle slightly, pointing toward the mountains in the distance.

"I take it that is where we must go?" Henri said.

"It is." Zenobia hobbled up the steps, helped as always by the faithful Farah. "Leave my staff where it is. It will protect your crew."

"Protect them from what, old mother?"

Zenobia pointed at the blazing golden orb of the sun directly above them in the sky. "Not for naught is Cobophia known as The Land of The Frozen Sun. In the days before the foundations of The Roof of The World were laid, Cobophia was. The birthplace of those who came before the gods. Time has no place here because it was here before time existed. The sun has not moved a fingernail's thickness from where you see it now. And as such, those few men who have come here know not how long they have stayed. Some men have come and returned home, swearing that they have been gone for years only to find that a few short days have passed. Others have returned home to find their own grandchildren aged and feeble with grandchildren of their own while they themselves have not aged a day."

"We will not suffer such a fate?" Omar demanded.

"If your men stay on the ship, with my staff they will be fine," Zenobia assured him. "As for the rest of us, I can protect us. But it will take all of my reserves of power to do so." Zenobia looked at Sinbad. "That is another

...forcing it right toward a giant head...

reason why I needed you and your crew, Captain Sinbad. It will be up to you and them to protect us all from any and all danger as I will not have the power to do so."

Sinbad nodded, turned the wheel. "I see a cove that we can harbor in. Omar, prepare my weapons and see that provisions are packed."

"Aye."

No man could say how long it took for them to get ready but eventually they were. Sinbad had exchanged his soaked garments for fresh ones, his scimitar scabbarded on his back, throwing knife in his sash. Henri Delacrois shouldered a quiver full of arrows and hefted his best bow. Tishimi had changed into her suit of tatami, that lightweight suit of folding Japanese armor that was best suited for work like this rather than her full set of armor. Ralf Gunarson held his great battle axe in one hand, his sword sheathed on his hip.

"And where do you think you're going?" Sinbad asked of Omar. The First Mate walked over to where they waited for a longboat to be lowered over the side. Zenobia and Farah were already in the boat. With Omar were three able crewmen: Ingis, Echik and Novorr. Sinbad knew them to be among the better swordsmen of his crew.

"With you, where do you think? These three come with us. It wouldn't hurt to have a few extra swords or three more strong backs."

Sinbad nodded. "Agreed. But you stay here, Omar. You job is to keep my ship and my crew safe. How many times have we…"

Omar gently cut Sinbad off; "Captain, I was a sailor before I was First Mate. And you cannot expect me to not set foot on fabled Cobophia myself after having come this far."

Henri made an elaborate show of there something being stuck in his ear. "Did I hear aright? Were you not the loudest voice against us coming here? And now you want to go? Do you not fear the crew will enjoy themselves without you aboard to spoil their merriment?"

Omar growled, "Close thy perfidious mouth lest I close it for thee! I speak to my Captain, not you!"

Sinbad sighed. "Suppose I agree. Who then do we leave in charge?"

"Haroun."

The air of Cobophia was filled with the raucous, uproarious laughter of the crew of The Blue Nymph. Haroun flushed with righteous indignation and leaped up on top of the railing and thumped his chest, "Aye, Haroun! And why not? Who among you dares say that I have not proved myself time and time again to be loyal to Sinbad and this ship! Indeed, I have sailed with Sinbad on many more voyages than some of you! I..."

"Enough, Haroun. Cease your posturing and come down from there. You look ridiculous." Sinbad ordered. The youth did so and Sinbad placed his hands on Haroun's shoulders. "And you are right. As is Omar." Sinbad raised his voice so that all could hear him. "First Mate Omar comes with me and Haroun is in charge. Let his word be as that of mine and woe be the son of misfortune who does not heed his orders!"

The crew of The Blue Nymph cheered and swore by the Eyes and Ears of The Prophet that they would obey Haroun. Sinbad winked and clapped him on the shoulder.

All this time, the remaining two Steel Leopards had stood off to one side, talking quietly to each other. Now Sinbad stepped to them. "As far as I am concerned you have performed the task charged to you. And I will swear to such when we return to Basra and you must report to Sokurah. If you wish to stay aboard The Blue Nymph you are welcome to do so and no man here will call you coward."

The Steel Leopards bowed as one. "If it pleases you, Captain Sinbad, we would join you and your companions. This adventure suits us."

Sinbad salaamed in return. "Join us and be welcome. What are your names?"

"He is Hanaj and I am Memohad."

And so a bigger longboat was selected and lowered over the side. Haroun and the crew watched as the three crewmen, along with Ralf rowed the craft and its occupants toward Cobophia. And there was not a one of them who did not offer prayers to Allah The Merciful and Compassionate for the safe return of all.

❀ ❀ ❀

Bavathi The Executioner watched from up high on the foredeck as his men rounded up the crew of The Honorable Wolf. The seamen had been rousted out of their beds roughly by Bavathi's mercenaries. The sea dogs of The Honorable Wolf were no cowards. They all had seen more than their share of battle. But they simply were no match against men who made their living by killing. They could see it in the glittering, blood lusting eyes of the mercenaries and so they allowed themselves to be herded like cows onto the main deck.

Iskosia appeared by Bavathi's side. The sorceress had regained her voluptuous form, her raven-black hair streaming behind her head like a proud flag in the stiff breeze. Gold and silver bracelets and anklets winkled in the torchlight. Her silken robes blew about her like multicolored smoke.

It was but an hour until dawn and their arrival at the Sea of Jade Mist.

Captain Zibo bawled from where he stood with his men. "We had a deal! You were to take my men and leave me alone!"

Bavathi shrugged. "A swine who would betray his own men is less than the dirt beneath my boot heel. Try and die like a captain at least." He turned to Iskosia. Bavathi would never dare mention it but he could see strands of ivory in the once pure ebony mane of hair. The backs of her hands were now slightly wrinkled where once they had been as smooth as the bottom of a Silacamian courtesan. The corners of her mouth trembled slightly when she thought no one was looking.

As if reading his thoughts, Iskosia turned to look full into his eyes and one hand went out to stroke his cheek. And even that brief caress made his blood boil with passion. "Do not trouble yourself so, Bavathi. Magic takes its toll on the user. And as I have no patron demon or god I must needs draw on my own inner reserves to power my spells."

"Will you have enough strength to get us to Cobophia?"

"I don't." Iskosia turned and pointed a long-nailed hand at the cursing, trembling sailors. "But they do. I have a way to get us there without using my own strength. Which I need to save to use against that old witch Zenobia when we finally meet for the final time." Iskosia held up something that sparkled in her hand as the first rays of the dawn struck it. "Behold, O Executioner. Is it not lovely?"

The object in her hand appeared to be a frog carved out of some milky, ancient crystal.

"I suppose it would fetch more than a few coins in the marketplace. Why?"

"I prepare to summon an ally who will take us to Cobophia. Warn your men to get back when the signal comes."

"What signal will that be?"

Iskosia's laughter was pure sweet foulness. "Oh, they will know, dear Bavathi. They will know."

As lightly as a girl on her bare feet, the jewels in the rings on her toes twinkling, Iskosia ran over to the railing, lifted the crystal frog to her lips and threw it in the water. She extended a long, slim arm and drops of light dangled from her fingertips as she muttered her incantations.

Bavathi turned his attention to his men. "Get ready. There will be a signal. When you see it you will know when to draw back."

"What will this signal be, O Executioner?"

"I don't..." Bavathi broke off. He had heard something like a gurgling rumble off the port side of The Honorable Wolf. He cocked his head to hear better. Iskosia contained to speak softly, her voice cajoling as if persuading something under the water to come up. And again Bavathi heard that gurgle. He stared forward, his right hand slowly going to the hilt of his great scimitar.

And then, with a tremendous splash of water, a massive webbed hand reached up and out of the water. It laid hold of the railing and was soon joined by another. And then nightmare hauled itself up out of the ocean.

An obscene amphibious horror it was. An unholy joining of man and frog in aspect. Water ran off its scaly back, arms and legs as it pulled itself over the railing and flopped to the deck. The horrendously wide mouth and goggling eyes seemed impossibly large for the misshapen head. The stink rolling off the creature made Bavathi gag. Small crawling things clung to the creature's hide and its obscenely long tongue flickered out to seize the things and yank them into the creature's mouth where it crunched on them as if they were the sweetest of tidbits.

Bavathi's men wisely judged that this must be the signal he spoke of and drew back. Most of the crew of The Honorable Wolf were too petrified with fear to move but some took advantage to leap over the side. But there was no succor there. Bavathi heard them screaming and thrashing as if the men were fighting something in the water. He looked to Iskosia for confirmation and she nodded. "Wor'shy'on always travels with his children and they must need be fed as well."

The abhorrent batrachian monster turned its broad, flat head toward Iskosia and spoke in a voice that sounded as if it were more used to speaking thousands of fathoms below the waves. "Thou hast used my totem to summon me, sorceress. Speak thy will. One request and one only may thou ask of Wor'shy'on."

"Then I bid thee take this ship and all aboard her to Cobophia! All save those mortals you see before thee as I offer their blood, their bones and aye, their very souls to you in tribute!" Iskosia pointed at the screaming, trembling crew of The Honorable Wolf.

With a great belching burp and a might spring, Wor'shy'on leapt upon the sailors. Bavathi had seen many a bloody slaughter in his years. Had himself participated in many more. But he closed his eyes at what he beheld. "Men should not have to die in such a manner," he whispered to himself.

Not soon enough, it was over and Wor'shy'on's appetite was sated, covered from head to webbed toes in gore. He held an arm in a malformed taloned hand, munching on the fingers as he slouched over to the railing. "It is a good and fitting tribute, sorceress. I will take thee and thy ship to Cobophia. You shall be there in the hour."

Bavathi watched gladly as the thing dived overboard. "Must we be in league with such demons?" he demanded.

"I would ally myself with Iblis himself if it secured me what I wish the most! The Well of Apollo and the power to reshape this miserable world to my will and word!" And the insane laughter of Iskosia filled Bavathi's ears as Wor'shy'on and his abominable children bore The Honorable Wolf to Cobophia.

The trail wound through the expanse of jungle. Surprisingly wide and clear, it was as if it had been cut only yesterday by expert woodsmen. Sinbad and Ralf took the lead with Henri and Tishimi bringing up the rear. Sinbad's crewmen, the two Steel Leopards, Farah, Zenobia and Omar were in the middle. No sound of animal or insect could be heard. Cobophia was as silent as a tomb as midnight. But the relentless sun beat down on them, the sun remaining high in the sky, never moving so much as a millimeter.

"A man could grow to hate a land of eternal daylight," Henri grumbled. "No night to spend pleasant hours with friends in a tavern or with a beautiful woman by a quiet fire."

Tishimi raised an eyebrow but said nothing.

"You would be a more agreeable companion if you talked more," Henri said. "I am not used to a woman who doesn't appreciate my conversation."

"And I am not used to a man who prattles on about every thought in his head as if they were the most precious pearls of wisdom," Tishimi answered.

Zenobia cackled and said, "Your friends must be bored, Sinbad, that they pick a quarrel with each other!"

"Aye, old mother," Sinbad agreed. "But if my guess is right, they may soon have others to pick a quarrel with." He pointed at the trail up ahead. It now sloped gently upwards, becoming a series of switchbacks that wound snake-like up the side of a hill toward the entrance to a cave. But it was what now lined both sides of the trail that caused Henri to nock an arrow in his bow and the others to loosen their swords in their scabbards. Horned and fanged skulls, bleached white in the eternal sun. Skulls bearing only one eye socket and easily three or four times the size of a human skull.

"What are they?" Hanaj wondered out loud.

"Cyclopses skulls," Sinbad answered.

"Are you sure?"

"Oh, trust me...I am sure."

"I only ask because I have heard the Cyclops are a race of giants!"

"They are. These are baby Cyclops skulls."

They continued up the trail, wondering at what could have been so vicious as to have killed so many infant Cyclopses and set their skulls as testimony to their skills at slaying the creatures. And where were the parents?

"Zenobia? What can we expect to find here? What manner of guardians?" Sinbad asked.

Before the old woman could answer, they all heard screams of rage above them. Sinbad looked up and the towering cliffs above the cave entrance. Long limbed naked men with large crimson eyes and gnashing fangs gibbered and danced on the edge of the cliff. Some threw rocks down upon them.

"Into the cave! Quickly!" Sinbad ordered. The group obeyed without question. Ralf Gunarson swept up Zenobia in his mighty arms and carried her. Once inside the cave, he set her down and unslung his axe from his back.

"Henri, Tishimi...watch our backs until we can light torches," Sinbad said. The archer nodded and took a knee, drawing back his bow slightly, half aiming at the cave entrance. Tishimi kept her hand on her katana. She did not draw the weapon unless she intended to use it and did not return it to the scabbard until it had drawn blood.

Ingis and Novarr carried sacks on their backs containing items that Omar thought would prove useful and the torches within certainly were that. Omar used flint and steel from his pouch and soon, five torches were lit and the band continued. The tunnel was unusual in that the curving walls were perfectly smooth. Sinbad wondered what artisans and with what tools had created such a tunnel with walls that felt like glass to the touch? This was truly a strange land. One in which he could easily spend years investigating its mysteries.

The tunnel branched off into three. Sinbad gestured to Zenobia. "Which way?"

The old woman looked at each tunnel in turn and then pointed at the middle one. "We go this way," she said firmly.

They continued on, the illumination of the torches providing a comforting aura of light around them. Presently, Omar nudged Sinbad.

"What do you make of this?" he asked. Omar held up his left arm. Omar's arms were extremely hairy and on the back of his arm, his hairs were all standing up.

"We are close!" Zenobia confirmed. "The Well of Apollo is not far! Come!"

They continued on, coming to a branch in the tunnel where it widened considerably, turning into a sweeping staircase that led them upwards into an immense chamber that might have been carved from the inside of an immense pearl, so gleamingly white was it. Their path was now lined by marble, gold and silver statues of men and women, all carven with such imagination and skill that it took their collective breath away.

"There's a fortune right here, Sinbad," Henri exclaimed. "You can keep my share of whatever the old woman's paying you! I claim one of these gold statues for myself!"

"And how would you get it back to The Blue Nymph, O greedy one?" Omar demanded.

"The strong backs of your bravos there…"

"My men are not here to carry…"

"Be silent, the both of you!" Sinbad commanded. "Do you not hear?"

And now that Omar and Henri fell silent they did hear. There was no adequate way to communicate the sound they were hearing. But they felt it. It was as if the sound reached into the very core of their souls and stirred memories of where they all had been before they were born. They continued on into an even larger chamber that might have been a cathedral designed a divine architect. The ceiling high above them shone with its own radiance that bathed them all in a gentle golden glow. Four statues some twenty feet tall stood at the four corners of the room and Zenobia bowed to each of them in turn. They were statues of women whose faces radiated immense wisdom and goodness. One held a scroll, the other a sword and shield. The third held a bowl of fruit and the fourth a jug.

Zenobia pointed to the center of the chamber. "There, my friends. We have arrived. Come and behold what you have travelled so far to find."

They all walked to the square step well located in the center of the chamber. One had to descend a short flight of stairs to reach the water. But as they all stood at the lip of the step well they could see immediately that what was within was not mere water.

What lay in the well moved and flowed and rolled like water but was as black as the intergalactic gulfs between the stars. And stars indeed looked as if what was contained within the ebony stuff in the well. Miniature

...their path was now lined with marble...

galaxies and nebulae swirled within the onyx depths. Solar systems and star clusters tumbled like cosmic dice in the pool of jet. An entire cosmos lay at their feet and none of them could speak or even breathe until Zenobia broke them out of the spell. "You look upon what mortal man has not seen in uncounted generations. You look upon The Well of Apollo which contains the very waters of the universe!"

"And very shortly it shall be I who bathes in those waters, old crow!" The triumphant voice of Iskosia rang out in the cathedral, rebounding from the silvery walls. As one, Sinbad and his loyal crew whirled to see Iskosia standing at another entrance, Bavathi the Executioner at her side. Like dark winged carrion birds, The Executioner's men spread out in a semi-circle on either side of Bavathi and Iskosia with their swords out, grinning wolfishly as they anticipated an easy slaughter.

"The game is over, Sinbad! And you have lost!" Bavathi boomed. "Stand aside and give way. I'll be lenient and give you and your men a clean death if you comply."

Sinbad's reply was just as booming and as confident. "It'll be I who sets the terms here, boastful one. If you and your men lay down your weapons and surrender, you'll be well treated."

Growls from Bavathi's men were equaled by the growls from Sinbad's crew.

Zenobia stepped forward. "This conflict is between us, Iskosia. Has there not been enough needless deaths? You know that you cannot bathe in these sacred waters. The calamity that would result would be catastrophic."

Iskosia strode forward. And as she did so, a remarkable thing happened. Her beauty faded. Her skin became wrinkled, mottled. Her lustrous raven black hair turned snow white. Her erect posture gave way to a hunched back. By the time she walked ten feet she transformed in a woman who looked easily as old as Zenobia herself.

"Iskosia! Beware! The witch works her magic on you to turn you into a crone like herself!"

Zenobia's youthful laughter rang out. "It is you who have been the victim of magic, fool! I never saw Iskosia as anything but the way she appears now! This is her true appearance and has been all along! She spends much of her power to create and maintain the illusion of youth and beauty, but here in this place of power she cannot! Behold your mistress in all her true unparalleled loveliness!"

Bavathi recoiled in utter horror as he looked upon the twisted hag that was truly Iskosia. He clenched his teeth so hard his men could hear them grinding together as his stomach bubbled and boiled in revulsion. The things he had done to her and the things he let her do to him.

Iskosia turned to Bavathi, one eye covered with a milky film. The other one that looked at him glittered with frantic vitality. "Listen to me, Bavathi! All I need do is bathe in the cosmic waters of The Well of Apollo and I will be in reality what the illusion was! All that you knew me as I was will be in truth as well as the most powerful mortal on the planet! With you at my side we can carve out an empire that will make that of Alexander's look like the village of ignorant savages! None can prevent us from making this world our plaything if we only slay these fools before us!"

"Then let the conversation cease and the battle begin!" Sinbad roared and charged forward. His crew were at his back as they took the fight to Bavathi and his men.

Omar ducked smoothly underneath the slash of a black-robed mercenary with an agility that belied his stocky frame and twisted with a litheness that would have wrung tears of envy from Shireen the dancer, his Mameluke sword licking out to take his enemy in the back of the neck, swiftly decapitating him.

Ralf charged in with that terrible Viking berserker rage that did not even make a pretense of defense. Ralf was all attack. He boomed terrible war songs to Tyr and Odin as his axe hacked and hewed and wherever it struck, blood fountained in great arcs.

Tishimi had no war cries or songs. She went about her slaying with a serenity on her lovely face that was unnerving it its own right. No elaborate swordplay was necessary for her. She simply moved through her foes and only one cut from her katana was necessary. Lopped off arms, legs and heads flew through the air, adding to the crimson hell of blood that filled this once holy place.

Only Henri Delacrois stayed back. But not because he was a coward. Henri's swordplay was so-so but when it came to archery, he was unmatched. He was most effective from a distance where his sharp eye could watch his friends' backs and cover them from sneak attacks from behind or slay his foes from a distance. One mercenary sought to stab Omar in the back with a dagger. Henri sent an arrow into the base of his skull. Omar waved his sword, covered in blood from tip to hilt at Henri in thanks.

Iskosia hobbled as best she could at Zenobia. Farah leapt in the way but was knocked aside by a hard swung bony fist. Old she was but Iskosia's strength was that of a far younger woman. Farah gasped in surprise as she hit the ground, heaving to draw in air.

Iskosia's gnarled hands wrapped about Zenobia's neck. "Why won't you die, you old wench!"

"Never! Not so long as evil such as yours remains to be fought in this world! I shall never die while your kind remains alive!"

The two old women grappled with each other, falling to the ground, rolling over and over as they battered and tore at each other's face and what was left of their hair.

Sinbad and Bavathi circled each other. Sinbad's scimitar looked woefully inadequate when compared to that huge blade of Bavathi's. But the weapon was most deceptive. As was the man who held it, grinning wolfishly at the larger man. "You have been proven to have lived a fool, Bavathi. Don't die as one."

"Insect! Beetle! Worm that you are! Truly you are the father of misfortune and disorder! If it had not been for your infernal meddling I would not be revealed to all as a simpleton! For hate's sake I spit at thee!"

"Truly it is written that the wise man does not complain at the consequences of his own stupidity."

Bavathi yelled like a wild man and came on in a rush, that great blade swing back and forth in lethal arcs of steel. Sinbad met each and every slash and swing with his own blade, turning aside Bavathi's attacks with nimbleness and strength. Sparks flew from their blades as they met time and time again, Sinbad's blade standing up against the bigger scimitar with no signs of breaking or bending. The Masters of The White Forge had done their work well with Sinbad's scimitar. The two men were both equal masters of their weapon. For all its size, Bavathi handled it as if it were as light as a weed. As due to the broadness of the blade, it was difficult for Sinbad to get past it to score a killing blow.

Novorr had died in that first mad charge, hacked down by three blades. But the men who slew him were quickly cut down by Hanaj, Ingis and Echik who waded in, their blades clashing with those of the mercenaries that replaced their slain foes. Toe to toe they stood, neither side giving an inch as the swords blocked and parried, the men holding them shouting and cursing and even laughing.

Sinbad ducked under a whooshing sideways slice as Bavathi attempted to cleave him in half. Bavathi allowed the momentum of his swing to spin him around in a complete circle. He angled the blade downward, thinking to cut Sinbad's legs out from under him. But Sinbad was no longer where he had been. He bounded upwards with the agility of a panther, back-flipping over the sweep of the broad blade and landing lightly well out of range. He tossed his scimitar from one hand to the other, that maddeningly insolent smile on his face.

Iskosia gained the upper hand, rolling on top of Zenobia. She seized Zenobia's head, lifted it up and slammed it back down on the ground. Zenobia yelled as her sight went away. Iskosia scrabbled for a nearby fist sized stone and lifted it, her intent being to smash Zenobia's skull to a pulp. She never completed the action due to Farah slamming into her with thunderous impact, throwing the old sorceress off Zenobia. The two women rolled over and over and ended up with Farah on top. She scrambled to her feet, yanking Iskosia to her feet as well. Iskosia spat, kicked, yammered ineffectual curses as she fought to get free. Farah drew back a small fist, swung and knocked Iskosia flying some ten feet. The old sorceress crashed to the ground in a small storm cloud of dust.

Sinbad's crew had made short work of Bavathi's men. There were only two or three left alive and they threw down their weapons, fell to their knees and in the name of Allah the Compassionate begged for mercy.

Sinbad and Bavathi continued their duel and it was rare indeed to see such a display of swordsmanship as the two men lunged, parried, blocked and riposted. Sinbad's scimitar whipped around his head and shoulders so quickly that it appeared he had more than one blade protecting him from the many overhand strokes that Bavathi delivered, his intention being to simply batter his opponent into submission. But there was much hidden strength in Sinbad's arms and shoulders and they bore the impact.

Bavathi tried to throw Sinbad off balance by switching swords from one hand to the other since like Sinbad he was at home wielding a blade with either hand but Sinbad was too canny for that and blocked the huge scimitar. And then their blades were locked at the hilts and the two men were nose to nose between their swords, stamping about in a circle, trying to gain the advantage.

"Your sorceress is defeated by a mere girl and your men have either surrendered or been slain," Sinbad said softly. "I give you a last opportunity to lay down your sword."

Bavathi snarled, "Thy maternal progenitor!"

Sinbad's eyes flashed with wrathful rage. He pushed away from Bavathi and renewed his attack. No longer did he smile, laugh or make jokes. This combat was now savage and determined. To Bavathi it seemed as if Sinbad suddenly had grown four more arms, all of them with a sword in their fists. And then one of those blades appeared to glide right past his defense.

Bavathi the Executioner fell to his knees, his huge sword dropping from a hand that no longer had the strength to hold it. He slowly fell forward on his face.

Omar walked up to Sinbad, who flicked blood off his sword. "What did he say to make you so angry there just before you killed him?"

"He spoke ill of my beloved mother. Who is still alive?"

Before they could take inventory, they all heard Henri's voice bellowing, "Hi! Stop that! Are you insane?"

They all turned to see Farah helping Zenobia hobble down the stairs toward the rolling ebony waters of the Well of Apollo. Sinbad and his friends ran toward them, shouting for them to stop.

They could all see Zenobia bestow a loving kiss upon Farah's forehead then the old woman just let herself fall into the black intergalactic waters. Farah scrambled back up the steps to face an angry Sinbad who seized her by the arm, roughly yanked her to her feet.

"Just what do you and the old woman play at? You told me that any mortal who dared bathe in the cosmic waters would unleash chaos upon the earth!"

But Farah grinned delightedly and replied, "Not so, brave captain! I told you that she who is sanctified by The Mother of The Phoenix may dive into the Well of Apollo. Stand back and behold!"

They did indeed draw back, watching as Zenobia swam to the center of the pool. She disappeared in those star laced obsidian waters.

"The old fool has caused many a needless death simply to drown herself," Omar muttered.

A geyser of silver radiance exploded upwards from out of the pool, cresting near the roof of the chamber, drops of diamond-like miniature flares raining down on Sinbad and his crew. They did not burn or sting as they anticipated but instead felt cool upon their skin. The silver radiance whirlpooled in the air and something emerged from it.

A beautiful woman of light with immense wings from which the fire of the stars dribbled. She smiled and such was the love and benevolence in that smile that Sinbad and his crew could only smile back.

"Greetings, my good friends. And especially to you, Captain Sinbad," the woman of light said.

"Who are you?" Sinbad asked.

"You knew me as Zenobia so why not continue to call me that? I doubt you could pronounce my true name, in any case." Zenobia giggled.

"And what are you?"

"I am the daughter of Rhysilis, The Mother of The Phoenix. Long ago I put aside the aspect you see me in now to live amongst my mother's worshippers so that I could understand them better. For thousands of years have I been on your world. Occasionally I would leave and travel the world. When I judged that enough time had passed that no one would remember me, I would come back to the abbey." Zenobia smiled. "It was most enjoyable to be one of you. The sensations and joys and sorrows of being human is like nothing else. My mother would occasionally call to me to come and rejoin her in her home beyond the stars. But the abbey needed me and I grew to appreciate being needed."

"You are akin to a goddess!" Ralf declared. "You did not need us!"

"Oh, no, dear barbarian. I am no goddess. Rather, think of me as a living being as different from you as you are from a cat. But thanks to the time I have spent as one of you, I like to think we are not so different. And I put aside much of my power to live as one of you as my human shell could only contain the smallest fraction of my power. But once Iskosia started with her schemes.." the wings flapped slowly. "I knew I had to come here and reclaim my power."

Zenobia reached out a hand and the still unconscious Iskosia rose into the air, floating over to Zenobia who wove a cocoon of energy around her.

"What will you do with her?" Sinbad asked.

"Give her what her heart desires," Zenobia said simply. She waved her hand again and the cocoon disappeared to reveal that Iskosia was once again young and beautiful. But now she was a statue. A statue of marble and silver that floated to join the other statues lining the path leading to The Well of Apollo.

"And now, my dear friends, it is time for me to depart. Farah, I bequeath to you Moonsilver Abbey."

Farah dropped to one knee and bowed her head. "Thank you for all you have done for us."

"Oh, no...thank you, dear Farah, for being my friend all these years. You have given me far more than I have given you." Those golden eyes turned toward Sinbad. "And thank you, Captain Sinbad. I could not have done this without you."

"Then may I ask you for something?"

"Certainly."

"I would like something to remember this adventure by. I always have something from one of my voyages to keep and there is something I would like from here."

"Name it."

And Sinbad did.

When Zenobia laughed it was the sound of the wind between the stars. "A most unusual souvenir, Captain Sinbad! But I would expect nothing less from you! It shall be done!" And just like that, it was. Sinbad had his souvenir in his hand.

Those wings of fire began to flap more strongly. "My staff will see you safely back through to waters that you know, Sinbad. For I must now bid farewell to you all," Zenobia called. "May whatever god you worship or whatever star you follow keep you safe! Farewell, dear friends! Farewell!"

And with a silent explosion of incandescence, Zenobia was gone.

The silence within The Great Hall of Cups was such that the footsteps of a cat would have sounded like thunder in the mountains if one had chosen that moment to walk by. Sinbad stood on the table, fists on hips, grinning at his audience.

"Say on, Sinbad! Don't leave off the story in the middle! What happened next?"

"What mean you 'what happened next?' Our task was done. We returned to The Blue Nymph and with the aid of Zenobia's staff returned through the Sea of Jade Mist, thence to friendly waters and then back to Basra. The surviving Steel Leopard, Hanaj, made his report to my friend Sokurah and asked if he could be discharged from service that he may join my crew. He was and he did. I myself escorted Mistress Farah back to Moonsilver Abbey where with the aid of myself and my friends, she quickly put things aright and took up her duties."

"Was she sorry to see you go, Sinbad?" Shireen called out, causing a storm of laughter to fill the common room. And none joined in the laughter more than Sinbad himself.

"Let us just say that I thought it prudent to leave her to her work and return to mine!" More laughter filled the room until the voice of Jamel Dreadbeard cut it down.

"But where is thy proof O master of adventure? Never before has Sinbad El Ari returned from a voyage without the proof of where he has been? Produce thy proof!"

Sinbad winked. "In truth, I am most delighted you said that, obtuse one. Behold!" Sinbad thrust a hand inside his sky blue silk shirt and removed something that lay in his palm. Sinbad's audience eagerly crowded to see what it was.

The size of an orange it was. A sphere black as obsidian. And contained within it they could see a multitude of stars. Miniature whirling nebulas and galaxies. A nimbus of cosmic clusters.

"I asked to be able to hold the waters of infinity in my hand, my brothers. And this is what Zenobia gave to me. And I show it to you. Look deep within, my friends! Look long enough and hard enough and you can see small worlds the size of a grain of sand! Who among you would dare say it is not possible that upon those grains of sand live men and women not unlike us? Who live and love, slay and strife, work and worry? Likewise it may be that the world we ourselves live in is in turn being held in the palm of an infinitely larger being?

"And that is why I wished for this, friends and brothers. To remind myself of the eternal mysteries of life. Aye, for every day brings new mysteries and new adventures. And some of them are as far away as The Land of The Frozen Sun while others are right in the palm of your hand."

Sinbad replaced the sphere in his shirt. "And now, I must be going! Omar insists on returning to the tedious chore of transporting goods even though the chests of gold and jewels promised to us rests safely on The Blue Nymph. The man is a tyrant, I swear!"

"Don't go, Sinbad! The night is young and there is wine aplenty! Tell us of another adventure!"

Sinbad regained his cloak, shaking his head regretfully. "Would that I could. But I fear that I have told you of all the adventures that I have had recently. Sinbad made to fasten his cloak but then paused as if struck with a sudden thought. "But now that I pause to think...did I ever tell you of my voyage to The Isle of Bronze? The island where the gods themselves store their treasures?"

The entire assemblage roared with one voice; "No!"

With a laugh, Sinbad threw away his cloak and leaped back up on the table. "Then pour the wine and fill all the cups! This will take a while! It was in The Month of The Ram that this voyage took place. My crew and I found ourselves in a most curious land called Colchis when..."

...but that is a story best left for another time. For this is the tale of Sinbad's voyage to The Land of The Frozen Sun and that voyage is done. But fear not, O my children. For Sinbad, his stalwart and true friends and the brave crew of The Blue Nymph had many more adventures and many more voyages. Stranger voyages and adventures than this one, if you can believe it! And you can. For is not Sinbad truly the prince of sailors and the master of adventure? And if it is the will of Allah the Merciful and Compassionate we next we meet, wherever it may be, it will be the honor of this humble servant to tell you of those voyages. And until then, in the words of Sinbad El Ari himself and by the Eyes and Ears of The Prophet I swear I heard him say this myself: "There is no end to the adventures we can have in our lives if we but seek them out."

The End

SIGNING
on with SINBAD

Why is it that some ideas sit around in the labyrinthine depths of my subconscious for days, weeks, months, even years and I never feel a particular urge to work with them, flesh them out and see if I can get a decent story out of them but other ideas seize me by the hair and refuse to let go until I pay attention? Never before had I thought of doing a Sinbad story until Ron Fortier threw out the idea of SINBAD: THE NEW VOYAGES. He was specific about two things. He wanted the appearance of Sinbad to be based on the actor Taye Diggs and he wanted the stories to be inspired by the trilogy of Sinbad movies co-produced by special effects master Ray Harryhausen.

I gotta admit, I was more turned on by the idea of writing my own prose version of a Ray Harryhausen movie than anything else. I appreciated that Ron was giving writers the opportunity to not only write a Sinbad that culturally/racially was far more accurate than what we've previously seen in movies and television. But I was more appreciative that I was getting a chance to stretch out a bit and explore a genre that I love but I haven't written yet. At least not professionally.

Way back when I first discovered Robert E. Howard, Charles Saunders, Michael Moorcock, Karl Edward Wagner, John Jakes and Lin Carter, my imagination was immediately fired by the rich lushness and savage testosterone fever of the sword and sorcery genre and as most young writers do, I started writing the stuff myself. I had more fire and imagination than skill but at that time I was writing to entertain myself so I didn't care. It was fun.

And that's what attracted me the most when Ron put this idea out there: fun. Despite what you may have heard, New Pulp ain't exactly making anybody rich. Although I do keep hearing rumors about that Barry Reese and an alleged gold plated Cadillac he owns. But for a poor slob like me, the grease that keeps my squeaky wheel turning is if a project is going to be fun and can I bring something unique to the project, a flavor that will make my contribution worth a reader's time and money. And I think that with "Sinbad and The Voyage To The Land of The Frozen Sun" I've done that. I certainly got to get my fun on as it was a blast to write a sword-and-sorcery tale. I'm known for writing modern day action-adventure spectaculars so it was a welcome change of pace to be writing about swords, spears and magic spells instead of martial arts and automatic weapons.

And who wouldn't want the chance to write about Sinbad? There's a reason he's known as Sinbad THE Sailor, y'know. I think that the only other sailor in popular culture who's more well-known is Popeye. But they both represent the same thing: the freedom of the open sea. The thrill of standing on the deck of the ship and knowing that just over that distant horizon lies new lands, new people to meet and above all, new adventures. And that's exactly what Sinbad represents to me…the eternal promise of new adventures every day and new horizons to sail beyond in search of even more wonders to see.

If you read carefully and if you're familiar with not only the Ray Harryhausen movies but also 1947 "Sinbad The Sailor" starring Douglas Fairbanks, Jr. as well as the 1940 "The Thief of Bagdad" you'll have spotted numerous references and homages to those films so I hope that enhanced your enjoyment of the tale.

And by all means, if you enjoyed this book then tell your friends to get hold of a copy and make sure you bug Ron as well. I've got a couple more voyages of Sinbad The Sailor I'd like to tell…

DERRICK FERGUSON – is a native of Brooklyn, New York which as all right thinking people know is The Center of The Universe. He's lived there most of his still young life. He has been married for 30 years to the wonderful Patricia Cabbagestalk-Ferguson who lets him get away with far more than is good for him.

His interests include radio/audio drama, Classic Pulp from the 30s/40s/50s and New Pulp being written today, Marvel and DC superheroes, Star Trek in particular and all Science Fiction in general, animation, television, movies, cooking, loooooong road trips and casual gaming on the Xbox 360.

Running a close second with writing as an obsession is his love of movies. He currently the co-host of the "Better In The Dark" podcast with his partner Thomas Deja and rants and raves about movies on a bi-weekly basis. "Better In The Dark" is a part of the Earth-2.net http://earth-2.net/ family of podcasts.

He is also a rotating co-host of the PULPED! podcast along with Tommy

Hancock, Ron Fortier and Barry Reese where they interview writers of the New Pulp Movement as well as discuss the various themes, topics, ebb and flow of what New Pulp is and why you should be reading it.

For further information about Derrick Ferguson, what he's up to and what he's going to do next we invite you to check out at your convenience these sites:

Blood & Ink http://dlferguson-bloodandink.blogspot.com/
Dillon http://dillon-dlferguson.blogspot.com/
The Ferguson Theater http://derricklferguson.wordpress.com/

HARRYHAUSEN SETS SAIL

by Ron Fortier

As much as I would like to tell you I first became aware of the Arabic hero Sinbad the Sailor in some literature class, I'd be lying. My introduction to that character of middle eastern origin wouldn't occur until long after I'd met him on the big silver screen at the local movie house in my hometown of Somersworth, N.H. The year was 1958 and I was twelve years old. The movie was *The 7th Voyage of Sinbad* and it starred Kerwin Matthews as Sinbad with Kathryn Grant as Princess Parisa, Richard Eyer as Barani the genie and Torin Thatcher as Sokurah the villain. I wish I could say I remembered it fondly, but honestly, Matthews just wasn't all that effective as a swashbuckling hero and the story's plot eludes me. What I do recall vividly was that the movie had some of the coolest stop-motion special effects ever and they were all the product of one Ray Harryhausen.

Now if you are one of the few people living on this planet unfamiliar with Mr. Harryhausen, shame on you. Here's a little bio to bring you up to speed. As a teenager, Harryhausen saw the classic 1938 *King Kong* and realized he wanted to know how all that movie magic was done. He proceeded to teach himself until finally he was hired by Willis O'Brien, the FX wizard responsible for the effects in the movie he had so loved. In fact Harryhausen so impressed his mentor that by the time 1949 came along, he was the chief FX Technician on O'Brien's final big gorilla epic, *Mighty Joe Young*.

But I digress here, our subject was Sinbad the Sailor and his cinematic debut in Harryhausen's film, *The 7th Voyage of Sinbad*. Although that movie, Harryhausen's fourteeth project, was a mild success, it really didn't break any box office records and he and his associates went on to bigger and better things. In the years that followed, he would oversea such FX classics as; *Mysterious Island, Jason and the Argonauts, First Men in the Moon, One Million Years B.C.* and *The Valley of the Gwangi*.

Now the same year his masterful *Jason and the Argonauts,* came out in 1963, a German film company produced and released *Captain Sinbad*, a movie shot in Bavaria and starring American actor, Guy Williams who would later gain fame as Zorro in the Walt Disney TV series and later as the father in the sci-fi *Lost In Space*. Unlike Matthews, the debonair and ruggedly handsome Williams made a memorable Sinbad. Joining him in this international cast were Heidi Bruhl as Princess Jan and Pedro Armendaris as the baddie, El Kerim. How successful this film was, I have no idea, but I have to believe it was seen by Harryhausen and must have rekindled some unrealized dreams he still harbored for the famed sailor of myth for eleven years later he would convince Columbia Studios to revisit Sinbad's world.

Thus in 1974, Harryhausen's second Sinbad venture, *The Golden Voyage of Sinbad* premiered with John Phillip Law as Sinbad. Although not as sophisticated as Williams, Law was a competent actor and gave the character a humorous panache that worked quite well. British actor Tom Baker took on the role of Koura the evil wizard, a job that would soon after help him land the part of Dr. Who on BBC. The beautiful Caroline Munro was the love interest with Takis Emmanuel as Achmed, Douglas Wilmer as the Vizier and Kurt Christian as Haroun. The movie was a hit from its opening weekend what with its deft mix of action, humor and stunning visual effects. Harryhausen's skills coupled with the evolution of film technology had grown in leaps and bounds during the sixteen years between his first Sinbad outing and this second. In scene after scene, his stop-motion magic awed viewers young and old alike.

Thus it was no surprise that the third Sinbad movie would arrive only three short years later, 1977 with *Sinbad and the Eye of the Tiger*. This time an energetic Patrick Wayne would take on the turban of Sinbad with the gorgeous Jane Seymour as Princess Farah, Margaret Whiting as Queen Zenobia and Kurt Christian as Rafi, Zenobia's son. The villain ironically enough was a former Dr. Who, Patrick Troughton as Melanthius. Although Wayne is clumsy in the role, even his stilted performance is easily overlooked by as yet another masterful romp enhanced by Harryhausen's wizardry making *Sinbad and the Eye of the Tiger* a fitting end to this cinematic trilogy.

There is no question amongst movie critics that none of these three were Harryhausen's best works, but they are fondly remembered by his legion of fans as terrific action adventure films that never took themselves seriously and totally entertained their audiences from their first scenes to their closing credits. What more can one ask of any movie?

So it was Ray Harryhausen who first introduced me to the colorful, exuberant sea going rogue known as Sinbad the Sailor and in these three films made me a life long fan. Thus last year, when deliberating on what kind of new series we at Airship 27 Productions could offer our loyal fans, Sinbad was one of the first heroes to pop into my mind.

I sat down and sent out a message to our gang of writers asking if anyone would be at interested in writing new pulp adventures of Sinbad? But I made it clear right from the beginning that we would not be taking on a scholarly approach to the hero via the *101 Arabian Nights,* heaven forbid. No way! Our Sinbad would be Ray Harryhausen's vision albeit with a few original tidbits of our own added to spice things up. The response was overwhelming and within a few days I had nearly a dozen writers signing on to write these stories, the first three to arrive on my desk you've hopefully had the fun of reading by now. We truly hope you had a good time, as much as we did bringing them to you.

And rest assured, volume two is already complete and won't be too far behind in coming your way and material for subsequent volumes is still coming in. This only goes to show you just can't keep a good pulp hero down, especially one with such a dynamic movie past.

Thanks for supporting us in this fun endeavor and we hope to see you back here for Volume Two of – *Sinbad : The New Voyages!*

Ron Fortier
7/1/2012
Fort Collins, Co.
(www.Airship27.com)
(Airship27@comcast.net)

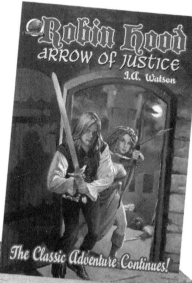

New Pulp scribe J.A. Watson brings his own vivid imagination to the Robin Hood saga, setting it against the backdrop of history but maintaining the iconic elements that have endeared the tale of Robin Hood to readers throughout the ages. With beautiful covers by fan-favorite artist Mike Manley and interior illustrations by award-winning artist Rob Davis, this is a fresh and rousing retelling of an old legend, imbuing it with a modern sensibility readers will applaud.

Airship 27 Productions is extremely proud to present —

Robin Hood

King of Sherwood • Arrow of Justice

DEATHWALKER

TOUCHED BY DEATH

While on his vision quest, the young Cheyenne brave High Bird encounters the sprit of Death. The powerful wraith recruits the boy as his new agent in the world and High Bird returns to his tribe altered forever as Deathwalker. When the Cheyenne become the target of a vengeful Pawnee Shaman, Stands Alone, only Deathwalker can stand between this evil sorcerer and the total destruction of his people.

Writer R.A. Jones has woven a new and exciting fantasy set against a background authentic Native American lore and culture. He dares to imagine what this wild untamed land would have become had there been no conquests by outside civilizations beyond the great waters. Here is an old world re-envisioned in a bold new action packed adventure worthy of pulp writers such as Robert E. Howard and Edgar Rice Burroughs. Featuring stunning cover art by Laura Givens with interior illustrations by Michael Neno.

Airship27 is proud to present R.A. Jones' DEATHWALKER, another original and quality title in the New Pulp movement.

Made in the USA
Lexington, KY
16 June 2014